RO'S
HANDLE

A Ro Delahanty Novel

DAVE LAGER

World Castle Publishing, LLC
Pensacola, Florida
Copyright © Dave Lager 2017
Hardback ISBN: 9781629897936
Paperback ISBN: 9781629897943
eBook ISBN: 9781629897950
First Edition World Castle Publishing, LLC, September 18, 2017
http://www.worldcastlepublishing.com

Licensing Notes

Anyone familiar with the western Illinois-eastern Iowa region will recognize Fort Armstrong County and Lee's Landing are loosely based on real places; "loosely" meaning I have taken significant liberties with the area's actual place names, geography, and history.

We've waited a long time for this, Nan
thank you for always being at my side

"We have an incredible warrior class in this country — people in law enforcement, intelligence — and I thank God every night we have them standing fast to protect us from the tremendous amount of evil that exists in the world."

Brad Thor

Table of Contents

Chapter One
Iowa's Best Shooter

Sunday, April 27, 2003, afternoon

Ro stepped up to the firing line, her left hand hanging relaxed next to her hip. She was glad she'd chosen her lighter, hip length, forest green denim jacket to conceal the Glock at her waist, as the Iowa Sportsman's Club indoor range was over air conditioned and a bit chilly. On the outskirts of Des Moines, it was known as one of the premier shooting facilities in the state and was hosting the first ever United States Sport Shooter's League (USSSL) Iowa state championship match.

The station judge, who was behind her a couple of paces and to her left, as that was Ro's shooting hand, raised his arm to signal the shooter at station eight was ready.

Three other station judges, two to her left and one on her right, had apparently done the same thing and the shooter's targets instantly popped up.

CRACK! Only two of the four remaining shooters actually fired, virtually simultaneously.

Ro's target, a guy in ski mask holding an AK-47, was clearly a bad guy; of course she drew and fired. The big scoreboard above the judge's table behind the firing line, not unlike the leader board at a golf match, said Ro's judge had awarded her nine points, which probably was for having been a smidgeon slow on the draw, because her shot on the target was dead center in the heart.

The other competitor who had fired — Roger Wheelan, a professional shooter — also obviously had had a bad guy as his target, although, because competitors couldn't see into adjacent firing lanes, Ro didn't know what his had been. The scoreboard said he'd also scored nine points.

The two other shooters — Adam Hicks, an amateur, and Doug Payne of the Iowa State Police — had received a surprisingly poor five points each. It was almost certain both shooters had made the same mistake; they had reacted a bit too quickly and partially drawn their weapons on what were really non-threatening targets. Being a little too fast on the draw for "a civvy," a civilian or non-threatening target, was a cardinal sin in sport shooting; the only worse mistake was in fact firing on a civvy.

"Sport shooting," as it was called, was a fairly recent addition to the firearms competition sphere. The idea was to simulate defensive shooting. Pop-up targets presented themselves unexpectedly; the target might be threatening or might not be. The shooter had to quickly distinguish which was which, then draw his or her weapon from a concealed-carry position and fire on the target. Points were awarded by a judge at each station for speed of draw and accuracy of the shot (i.e., in a kill zone); but drawing on or firing at a non-threatening target was a huge no-no, and resulted in big point deductions.

A USSSL sanctioned match included three rounds, usually conducted over three successive days, again similar to a golf match. Each round involved ten individual shooting stations. Each station was worth ten points; a round was worth one hundred points and a complete match was worth three hundred points: The shooter closest to three hundred at the end of the three rounds was the champion and earned the title of Best Shooter.

The four shooters left to complete the Iowa championship's third and final round were:

- Adam Hicks of Council Bluffs, Iowa: A roofer by trade, he was proving to be a surprisingly good amateur. Shooting with a Glock 35, the forty caliber version of Ro's nine millimeter Glock 34, Hicks had been in station ten, to Ro's far left, and had just completed his final round.
- Doug Payne of Pine Grove, Iowa: A lieutenant with the Iowa State Police, he favored a Smith & Wesson M&P 40. Payne had just completed his ninth station to Ro's immediate left.
- Ro Delahanty of Lee's Landing, Iowa: A dispatcher with the Fort Armstrong County Sheriff's Department, she was representing the Witness Tree Rod and Gun Club and had just finished her eighth station.
- Roger Wheelan of Valdosta, Georgia: A full-time professional shooter, he was shooting a Kimber Gold Match II 45. Wheelan, immediately to Ro's right, had just finished his seventh station.

At the end of Saturday's second round Ro and Wheelan were tied for the lead with 178 points each; Payne was only a point behind at 177; while Hicks had just 157 and seemed to be out of the running for a top spot finish.

However, so far Hicks was having an outstanding final round, scoring mostly nines and tens, while Payne was struggling, scoring only two points on one station and garnering a zero on another, which probably meant he'd fully drawn down on a "civvy." For all intents and purposes he and Hicks were now even, battling for the third place trophy.

Meanwhile, throughout the final round Ro and Wheelan had been going head-to-head, exchanging the lead several times.

After each station, competitors customarily turned to check the scoreboard on a raised dais ten yards behind the firing line. Ro had earlier spotted where her father, Big Mike Delahanty, and Johnna Mack, her coach, were standing together in front of the dais, along with several dozen other onlookers; at this point, sport shooting was more of a participant's sport than a spectator's sport.

It had been Big Mike who'd first introduced his daughter to skeet shooting at the Witness Tree Rod and Gun Club when she was fifteen-years old. She'd taken up handgun competition on her own when she was seventeen, eventually winning an Iowa state fixed target championship with a Ruger Mark II Competition 22.

But it had been a seminar held by Johnna Mack two years ago here at Iowa Sportsman's that had introduced Ro to sport shooting, which she'd immediately gravitated to because she saw it as an essential skill needed to help fulfill her ambition to become a cop. An ambition that was soon to be realized, as in July, after she'd reached the mandatory minimum age of twenty-one for deputies and completed her eight-week police academy training, she was slated to be sworn-in as a rookie Fort Armstrong County deputy sheriff.

Over those two years Ro had attended other sports shooting workshops conducted by Mack, a full-time professional shooter, and Mack had become something of a friend and informal coach.

Ro gave the pair a brief nod, which her father returned with a wink. Mack gave Ro a thumbs-up sign and, at the same time, mouthed silently, "Stay cool." That had been her final, in fact, only advice just before Ro had stepped into the first station for the initial round on Friday. As the Iowa Sportsman's host club pro, Mack was not eligible to enter the competition, for which Ro was grateful, since as far as she was concerned Mack would have won easily.

The updated scoreboard said:

- Hicks had completed his final round with eighty-eight points, for a total of 245 out of 300 for the match, a respectable if not necessarily outstanding score.
- At the end of station nine Payne had only sixty points for the round and a total of 237 for the match. He needed at least an eight in his final station to tie Hicks, a nine or ten would garner him sole possession of third place.
- At the end of her eighth station Ro had seventy-three points for the final round and a total of 251 points so far for the match.
- Wheelan's score through seven stations was 64, bringing him to 242 for the match; he and Ro were pretty much dead even.

Payne, Ro, and Wheelan each moved to the next station to their left and readied themselves. Now just three judges gave the signal the remaining shooters were ready.

Look at the hands, Ro reminded herself, with a slight smile. During one of Mack's seminars it's what she had told everyone: "Look at the hands of your target, they'll tell you everything you need to know about whether it's a threatening or non-threatening target. Most shooters waste too much time looking at the face or trying to scan the whole body."

Ro smiled because it was so much like what her sensei used to tell her about competing in judo: "Watch your opponent's shoulders. They will signal to you what he intends to do. If he cocks one shoulder, it means he's going to attack with the opposite hand; if he throws one shoulder back, it means he's going to try a kick with the opposite foot." It had helped Ro advance to a black belt level and win more than a few judo competition trophies.

CRACK-ack! Only two of the three remaining shooters fired, with one just a split second behind the other.

This time Ro's target appeared to be a pre-teen male holding a gun in a threatening position, like he was about to fire, except the "gun" was in truth a lime green plastic water pistol. Immediately recognizing it as a non-threatening target, Ro stood absolutely still, not even twitching her fingers. Apparently the judge was impressed by her coolness, because when she turned to check the scoreboard there was a ten posted next to her name.

While Payne's target had apparently been a bad guy, it must have been tough to discern, as even though he had drawn and fired he must have noticeably hesitated; the scoreboard showed only seven points.

Meanwhile, Wheelan, like Payne, must have gotten a really tricky bad guy target; well this *was* a championship round, so there had been more than a few "tricky" targets along the way. His score was a seven, ordinarily not a major mistake, but in this case it turned out to be very costly.

At the end of the round:

- With the seven in his tenth station, Payne completed the match with 244 points, allowing Hicks to sneak into third place with a one point lead at 245.
- With her ten in the ninth station, Ro's score so far in the final round was eighty-three, putting her at 261 for the match.
- Whelan's six points put him at seventy through eight stations and at 248 for the match.

Ro and Wheelan moved to their left and readied themselves. The match was now almost out of reach for Wheelan; he needed to complete his two final stations with at least a pair of nines, and more importantly, Ro had to have a disastrous final station to give him a shot at the title of Iowa's Best Shooter.

As Ro stepped up to the firing line, the crowd's muttering, the judge's shuffling into position, the sound of Wheelan stepping up to his firing line, even the whirring of the mechanisms that moved the targets into position and popped them up all faded; there was just her hand relaxed and hanging down next to her left hip near her Glock and her eyes fixed on where the target would appear.

The target started to pop-up, except for Ro it was coming up in slow motion.

Her shot and Wheelan's were a split second apart: CRACK-ack! Ro's was first.

"Jesus," muttered the judge under his breath, although Ro didn't hear it.

At first glance Ro's target might have looked innocent enough, a mother holding a baby, except by focusing on the hands Ro quickly recognized the "mother" was holding the "baby" all wrong. A real mother cradles a baby with both arms, instead this "mother" seemed to be trying to balance the baby-like bundle on one hand while her other hand had disappeared inside the package…it was a suicide bomber!

In fact, the target had been a little over halfway up when Ro saw all she needed to see, drew, and fired, which is what brought the involuntary exclamation from the judge: Ro had drawn and fired in barely over one second, a phenomenal time.

However, because the target was still moving into position, while Ro's shot *was* a killing shot, it apparently had been just a tad off, as the scoreboard said she'd been awarded nine points in her last station, thus completing the final round with a very strong ninety-two points, putting her at 270 out of 300 for the match.

With just 248 points at the end of his eighth station, even

if Wheeler had gotten a perfect ten on his just completed ninth station, which he hadn't, and another ten on his yet to shoot last station, he still couldn't win.

Ro Delahanty was Iowa's Best Shooter!

Chapter Two
Deputy R. Delahanty

Tuesday, July 8, 2003, morning

Ro stood at the end of her bed, hands on her hips. In the background the CD player on one end of her low dresser was quietly playing Mozart's "Jagd" String Quartet, a short stack of other classical CDs nearby. She never listened to the radio, and rarely turned on the TV except to watch a movie or catch the news and weather just before going to work.

Taking in a deep breath and letting it out with a sigh, she turned and announced to the nearly three-foot tall black and white panda bear that looked on from his honored perch atop the other end of the dresser, her voice a kind of husky alto: "Well, Peter, it's happening…I'm really gonna be a *cop!*"

Peter Panda had been a gift from her Uncle Richard and Aunt Eileen—her mother's brother and his wife—on her second birthday. He had immediately joined her in her bed, only moving to the dresser in her sixth or seventh year. While a parade of other gift dolls—Aunt Eileen had no doubt thought every little girl just *loved* playing with dolls—had followed on birthdays and Christmases, including lots of Barbies and Barbie accessories, all

15

of which ended up in Ro's closet, mostly unopened, Peter Panda had never been deposed as her favorite.

He was clearly well-loved and well-worn, with several bare spots in his fur and one corner of his mouth missing, giving him a permanently crooked and somewhat inscrutable smile.

The queen bed, which nearly filled the small room, was situated facing a large window that looked out over a green wall of trees behind Ro's apartment. Above the bed were two large framed Ansel Adams black and white posters: "Oak Tree, Sunrise" and "Birds on the Beach."

She was looking down at her new Fort Armstrong County deputy sheriff's uniform neatly arrayed on the bed's light blue corduroy bedspread. Up by the pillows was her long-sleeved khaki shirt, with its chocolate brown pocket flaps and epaulets, an American flag sewn on the right shoulder, the Fort Armstrong County seal on the left, her plastic name badge—*Deputy R. Delahanty*, which she read with a smile of pride—pinned over the right breast pocket and the five-pointed star deputy's badge pinned above the left breast pocket.

Across the middle of the bed were her neatly pressed and creased chocolate brown trousers, with a khaki stripe down the outside of each leg. She'd been quite insistent with the uniform shop attendant about wanting a *men's* 28/33 size trouser, because that's what looked best on her slender, long legged, virtually hipless and buttless runner's frame.

Near the bottom of the bed were a dark brown baseball cap, with "Deputy Sheriff" in gold block lettering across the front, a pair of black socks and her over-the-ankle, dark brown tactical boots.

And, of course, the dark brown leather kit belt, with its empty holster on the left side—her departmental issue Sig Sauer P229 .357 was locked in the gun safe across the hall in the larger bedroom she used as her study—holders for two extra magazines, double handcuff case, cell phone case, mini LED flashlight case, radio, collapsible baton case, and in the center, where it would rest in the small of her back, an Uncle Mike's All-Purpose pouch to hold her wallet, keys, a small coin purse and a small slide-out gravity knife. Ro did not like bulging pockets.

"No, Peter," she said, correcting herself with a brief head shake. "Officially I'm not *gonna* be a cop, I *am a cop.*"

Except to her it didn't quite feel like it yet, even though yesterday afternoon Sheriff Mark Ballard had administered the deputy's oath in his office at the courthouse and issued her badge, photo ID, sidearm, radio, and kit belt. Because Ro Delahanty knew in her heart she wasn't a *real* cop until she put on that uniform, climbed into a black and white Crown Vic patrol car, and put herself in harm's way *out there.*

With a kind of wry grin, she recalled how her classmates had sniffed mockingly and rolled their eyes when she had pretty much said that same thing in Mr. Singer's fifth grade language arts class a little over ten years ago. The class was about to read Mark Twain's *Huckleberry Finn*, and Mr. Singer was introducing to the class the concept of symbols in literature. As examples, he showed overheads of the Statue of Liberty as a symbol of opportunity to millions of immigrants, and of a cross, a Star of David, and a crescent and star as symbols of three of the world's major religions.

Then he'd asked the class if they could think of any other kinds of everyday symbols.

After a few seconds of silence, somebody tentatively mumbled, "A stop sign?"

"Yes," Mr. Singer had said with enthusiasm, hoping to encourage more responses. "That's definitely a symbol for traffic laws. But you're missing a really big one right here in this room." After another few seconds of silence, he added, "I'll give you a hint: It's known around the world as a symbol of freedom."

17

"The flag!" came several overlapping responses, everyone glancing up at the American flag hanging from a short pole in a back corner of the classroom.

"Right!" he affirmed. "But come on, I've given you some easy ones. There are lots more if you just use your imaginations a little."

After another short silence, Ro raised her hand and Mr. Singer nodded, "Ro?"

"A police car," she'd said. She was picturing in her mind the black and white Lee's Landing squad cars she frequently saw around town.

"Cops! All *they* do is hassle people," someone muttered sarcastically from the back of the room. There were several snickers of agreement.

"No, no...," Mr. Singer said, gesturing with his hand to quell any more snarky remarks. "Why do you say that, Ro?"

"Whenever I see a police car it makes me feel better, like someone's there to...to...." She frowned, struggling for the right words. "To be there when there's trouble...like stopping bad people, or helping in a disaster."

Mr. Singer looked at her for a second or two and just nodded, like he understood completely but didn't have to say it.

And then, without ever having consciously thought about it before, Ro straightened up in her chair, squared her shoulders, and added with a self-assurance that surprised even her, "*I'm* going to be a cop someday."

And over the ten years since then she had never once strayed from that aspiration.

"Well," the now grownup Ro said aloud to Peter. "*Someday* is almost here, so let's get to it."

Turning, she pulled off her usual around-the-apartment T-shirt and cut-off sweats and headed for the shower.

Half an hour later she stood in front of the full-length mirror that served as the bedroom's closet door, now in full uniform. She liked what she saw, at least insofar as the uniform went. At five-ten-and-a-half she was tall and erect, her wide shoulders square. She'd bloused her shirt slightly at the waist to help mask her 34 C bust line. She'd combed and moussed her short, brick-red hair flat and straight back so no stray curls peeked out from under her deputy's cap. The uniform's overall impression was exactly what she'd hoped for: authoritative and professional.

But then there was the face.

Definitely her father's daughter, everything about her face said "Irish," from the strawberry blond brows to the big blue eyes, from the pushed-up nose and high cheekbones to the bow mouth and sharp chin. Except the proportions were just slightly off, so she'd never thought of herself as "pretty" Irish, more like "just plain" Irish. But she was still clearly "girl" Irish, a look she could not permit.

Looking over at the teddy bear, she raised an eyebrow, as if to silently say, *Here goes*, and then put on what she thought of as her "cop face."

It was a look she'd begun cultivating when she gotten her job as a night dispatcher with the Fort Armstrong County Sheriff's Department not quite two years ago. It included slightly clenching her teeth so her mouth was pressed into a thin, straight line—she never wore lipstick, or for that matter, eye makeup— and knitting her brows into a slight frown, which had the effect of narrowing her eyes. While it didn't entirely hide the fact she was a *female* police officer, it most definitely sent the message this was a *no nonsense female* police officer.

Happy with the look, she picked up the Sig she'd retrieved from the gun safe and dropped it into her holster, its two-pound weight settling comfortably on her hip. As a competitive shooter, she was quite used to the feel of a sidearm at her side.

"Peter, say hello to *Deputy* Delahanty," she said to the teddy bear, snapping off a salute.

And while she, of course, knew the stuffed animal had no muscles with which to change its perpetually benign facial expression, there was also no doubt in her mind Pete winked in approval.

***

"Hey, Deputy," a familiar, slightly gravelly voice called from across the parking lot behind the fortress-like, 1950s-era addition to the ornamental, 1890s-era county courthouse that served as the jail and sheriff's department.

"Girl, look at *you*," said Gwen Teague, eyeing Ro up and down, "all serious and *b-a-d*!" An African-American in her 40s, she was going to be Ro's replacement as an 11 to 7 shift dispatcher.

She held up her hand for a high five, which Ro returned.

"Thanks," Ro said. "I wonder what the other *deputies…*," she paused, raising an eye brow slightly, making it clear to Teague she meant what the "male" deputies, because, in fact, all of the other deputies in the department were male, "…are gonna think?"

Teague gave a half derisive, half droll snort. "Hah! There're a couple of Neanderthals who'll grump, you know that. But most of these guys respect you. It'll be fine."

Ro had been a fulltime night dispatcher for the sheriff's department for nearly two years, while Teague had been a part timer. Since they were both "new," at least in their respective jobs, they were on their way to a mandatory half-day new employee's orientation.

Even though the announcement letter for the orientation had said dress was casual, Ro had opted to wear her full uniform, feeling she needed to make a statement.

While as a dispatcher she knew most of the deputies and they knew her, including her ambition to become a deputy, this was the first time she would be meeting them in uniform, as a supposed equal; except, she worried…would *they* feel that way?

20

It wasn't like she would be the first female deputy in Fort Armstrong County. There had been two previous females; in fact, she had known them both. They'd lost one to marriage and motherhood, while the other had been recruited away by the Iowa State Police.

Ro used her card key to open the staff entrance, and she and Teague passed down a short hallway leading into what everyone referred to as "the bullpen." Located behind the reception counter, it was definitely from the 50s, narrow and long, with a high ceiling and rows of fluorescent tubes hanging overhead. And it was crowded with half-a-dozen desks for the various sergeants, a row of computers the deputies used against one wall, and, on the opposite wall, a table with a big coffee urn and a variety of mismatched mugs.

Sergeant Cyril "Pops" Waters was the first to notice Ro. He was at his desk typing something into a computer when he glanced up. A near forty-year veteran of the department, he was called Pops because as the department's training officer, he was a kind of mentor and father figure to new deputies. His kindly gray eyes and lined face broke into a big grin and he gave Ro an exaggerated thumbs-up sign.

So far so good, Ro thought. *But Pops is easy, he always encouraged me about becoming` a deputy. And anyway, he's* supposed *to like new deputies.*

Deputy Ricardo "Cowboy" Matero, who was getting a cup of coffee from the urn, was the next one to see Ro. On the force for a little over three years, he was, like Ro, a third shift patrol officer…except his duty days were Wednesday through Sunday, so what he was doing there on a Tuesday in uniform wasn't apparent. Clearly of Hispanic heritage, handsome and single, he liked to flirt with the young female dispatchers, receptionists, and administrative aides, but had never flirted with Ro, which she'd always appreciated.

Without the slightest hint anything was different, Matero held out the coffee mug he had just drawn from the urn.

"Coffee, Deputy?" he said, with only the barest emphasis on "deputy," but with not a trace of sarcasm or mockery. In fact, it seemed to Ro it was his casual way of acknowledging her new status, but without making an embarrassingly big deal out of it.

Appreciating the gesture, she took the cup and, deciding to take the plunge, with a nod said, "Thanks, Cowboy," using his deputy's handle for the first time ever.

Matero grinned broadly, in effect saying it was okay.

As a dispatcher, Ro not only knew the deputy's given names, she knew the nicknames or handles they'd received as deputies, conferred on them by their fellow deputies and which only deputies used to refer to one another. Matero was "Cowboy" because he'd grown up in Texas and was a big fan of the Dallas football team, even sporting a Cowboy's logo bumper sticker on his car.

So far so good with number two, Ro thought to herself.

Just then Bruce Battisen—called "Bats" because it had been an easy contraction of his last name—emerged from the adjacent deputy's ready room, his two-hundred-plus pound bulk lumbering between the closely spaced desks. What he was doing there in uniform was also a mystery, as he hadn't been on duty the night before. His schedule, the schedule Ro would be taking over, was Tuesday through Saturday.

He held out his hand. "Glad to see you made it," he said to Ro.

Ro took his hand. "Corporal," she said, using his rank instead of his deputy's handle. She ignored what might have been an implied put down, like he had somehow expected her to chicken out, instead taking it to mean he was "glad" because she was his replacement and he was anxiously looking forward to his retirement.

Battisen had been a deputy for twenty-six years, dating from the former sheriff, Lefty Struve's era. Ro was going to spend the next week, starting tonight, riding with Battisen to familiarize herself with her assigned patrol district, the western part of the county.

"Do you want me to pick you up somewhere later?" Battisen asked Ro, meaning with his patrol car at shortly before eleven to begin their first shift together.

One of the changes Sheriff Ballard had made when he'd been elected in 1992, he was nearing the end of his third term as sheriff, was to have deputies take their patrol cars home and to begin and end their shift from there, rather than always having to come into headquarters.

"That's okay," Ro said. "I'll meet you here at 10:45."

"Okay," Battisen said with a short nod.

Another deputy, Terry Didian—whose nickname was "Garth" because he liked to do Garth Brooks covers on karaoke—had followed Battisen into the bullpen. Didian was a second shift deputy, so what he was doing there at roughly the beginning of the first shift wasn't clear either. Except Ro knew deputies often found excuses, some legitimate, some not so much, to come by the office…something needed checking on the patrol car, they needed to talk to one of the sergeants for some reason, there was an HR matter that needed attention….

On the force for eight years, Didian reminded Ro a little of her brother, Tuck, good looking in a boyish kind of way and very social. He was married and had a kindergarten age son.

Stopping in front of Ro, he exaggeratedly looked her up and down, and with a deep frown said, "I don't get it, Deputy," first pointing at her, "you're wearing the exact same uniform," then pointing at himself, added, "that I am, but somehow it looks a *whole* lot better on you."

"That's 'cause Deputy Delahanty's got more class in her

little finger than you've got in your whole body, Garth," teased Matero, reaching out and yanking at the tail of Didian's uniform shirt.

Deputy Delahanty....

Okaaaay, Ro thought to herself with something that felt a little like liberation. She glanced at Teague, who just nodded, but with a knowing grin.

CHAPTER THREE
ENCHILADAS AND SOPAPILLAS

Tuesday, July 8, 2003, afternoon and evening

After the orientation, Ro drove back to her apartment, took off her uniform, carefully hung it up in her closet, and laid down for a nap, not bothered by a thunder shower that passed through around three. Working the dogwatch shift five nights a week as a dispatcher, then having two "regular" days off, she'd trained herself to take short naps and to wake up at specific times. She got up at four, took another shower, put her uniform back on, and was now headed to her parents for a celebratory dinner. While celebratory dinners were a tradition with the Delahantys, they were also a perfect excuse for her father, Big Mike Delahanty, to try something new in the kitchen.

The neighborhood where Ro grew up was a classic 1970s era collection of several dozen split-level homes on each side of York Ridge Lane, ending in a cul-de-sac. Cookie-cutter to the max, they all had the exact same lot dimension—eighty feet wide by a hundred and twenty feet deep—the exact same four-level, three bedroom, two-and-a-half-bath interior layout; the garage and driveway in the exact same position; even down to the single maple tree—now, after thirty years, finally looking like a real tree—in the center of every front yard.

The original developer had made some effort at individualization, using different treatments for the portico over the front door and/or a variety of exterior coverings...faux stone for some, faux brick for others, and varying combinations of colored siding. And, over the years, some owners had made their own efforts at uniqueness, adding shrubbery or small flower gardens, or, like her father, a deck across the front.

As she rolled down York Ridge Lane, Ro saw her dad's familiar ten-year old, beat-up F-150 and her mom's big red Expedition in their usual spots in the driveway. But what brought a smile to her face was the bright, goldenrod yellow Miata convertible parked alongside the curb, with her brother Tuck at the wheel and her mother, Kate, and dad, Big Mike, standing beside it in the grass.

Kate was still in her pants suit...it was one of her favorites, the one she called "my fox hunting suit;" black slacks flared at the ankle over black boots and a bright red jacket sporting a hunting horn-motif pin on the collar. She clearly had just arrived from her office where she ran Kate Delahanty Design, a commercial interiors studio. The contrast between her parents, even after all the years of growing up with them, still struck Ro.

Mike was, indeed, Big Mike; six feet two and close to two hundred and thirty pounds. And he looked every inch the Irishman, with ruddy cheeks, merry, bright blue eyes, a bow mouth that smiled easily, and a thatch of tightly curled, carrot-colored hair he kept cut short in what he called his "Irish 'fro." Ro was very much her father's daughter.

Big Mike had, of course, changed into his usual worn, but not ratty, jeans and sport shirt, worn outside of his pants. And he towered over his five-foot four-inch, maybe a hundred-and-twenty-five pound wife. Even at forty-six, though perhaps a bit more mature, Kate was still the drop-dead beautiful cheerleader-homecoming queen she'd been in high school. She wore her dark hair, a legacy from her Hispanic mother, in a short casual flip, although out here in the sunlight Ro could easily spot the gray strands beginning to appear.

"Tuck"—christened Patrick Sean—was Ro's older brother by two-and-a-half years. As an infant she'd had trouble saying "Patrick," instead it came out "Tuck," a nickname between brother and sister that stuck: "Patrick" to his parents, "Pat" to his friends, and "Tuck" only to Ro.

Favoring his mother's fine features, Tuck had boyish good looks and an easy charm that made him popular all through school. Where Ro was reserved, tended to take herself too seriously, and had only one good friend who wasn't a relative, Tuck was gregarious, had loads of dates, and many male friends. Yet, despite—or maybe because of—their personality differences, they'd been constant playmates as children and still remained close as adults, though there was still plenty of sibling banter.

Clearly Tuck had arrived only moments before his sister. He was still wearing his plaid sport coat—this one with a garish orange and green pattern—that was his trademark as an ad sales rep for KLEE-TV, the top station in the area, although he'd loosened his dark tie. On anyone else the plaid sport coat might have looked ridiculous, but somehow Tuck pulled it off with aplomb.

He'd reached across the car, opened the passenger side door, and was apparently trying to coax his mother into going for a ride, which she was declining with emphatic shakes of her head and palms held out.

Pulling her red Explorer—a much appreciated hand-me down from her mother—to the curb on the opposite side of the street, Ro opened the driver's door and stepped out. Knowing it was the first time her family would see her in uniform, she decided to make it a dramatic entrance. Stopping in the middle of the street, she put on her stern "cop face," eyes hidden behind aviator sun glasses, and placed her hands on her hips with legs slightly spread. It was not lost on her she looked more than a little like the good guy sheriff from an old Western movie about to face down a villainous gunfighter on the town's dusty main street as the townsfolk looked on.

Tuck, who'd climbed out of the sports car, frowned. "I *used* to have a sister who drove a car just like that. What happened to *her*?"

"She was snatched. I'm her pod person replacement," Ro answered in an as emotionless a monotone as she could muster, trying hard not to grin, referencing one of their favorite scary movies as kids, "Invasion of the Body Snatchers;" the 1978, Philip Kaufman version, of course.

But then Tuck's frown took on a more serious look. "Jeez, Ro," he said, looking her up and down and shaking his head slowly. "I *know* you're my *sister* standing there in front of me, but somehow you're a completely *different* sister than I remember growing up with."

"Thank you, Tuck," Ro said, quite seriously, taking his comment as a compliment. "I *am* the sister you grew up with, but I *do* hope I'm also a different sister, or all this," she gestured up and down her uniform, particularly stopping at the big holstered semi-automatic at her left hip, "...all this is bullshit."

Meanwhile, Mike and Kate had moved around behind the sports car. Big Mike was smiling that oh-so-familiar smile of his, full of Irish amusement, full of love and pride, like he was saying, but not actually verbalizing, "Look at *you*! Little Ro ain't so little anymore."

Kate was just slowly shaking her head from side to side, as if she couldn't really believe what her eyes were telling her. "I hope you know how proud of you I am," Kate whispered, clasping her daughter's shoulders, needing to stand on tiptoe to reach her ear.

"I know, Mom," Ro whispered back, pulling her mother even closer into a full hug, wanting to emphasize the "I know."

As a child Ro had mostly been her daddy's girl. It was in her daddy's big recliner where she wanted to be read to sleep, although it was Kate who then usually carried her daughter to bed, tucked her in, and sang her a song in a clear soprano voice. It was her daddy she always preferred to hang out with. It was her daddy's old .410 shotgun she'd first learned to shoot with.

Only when she was a teenager and had experienced her first lover did Ro find a new connection with her mother, but more like a trusted older sister and confidant than mother-daughter.

"Hey," Big Mike said after a moment, "give the old man a chance here," gently prying his wife and daughter apart. But instead of hugging Ro, he stood back, gently removed her sunglasses, and looking into his daughter's eyes said with a big chuckle, "A *cop*. Cool!"

Ro's "cop face" quickly dissolved and she was, at least for a brief moment, once again Mike and Kate's little girl, basking in their delight for her accomplishment.

As they headed toward the front door, Ro stopped behind the Miata and gestured, "My god, Tuck, that's gonna be an even bigger girl magnet than the Sebring." When he was seventeen his parents had bought him a used Chrysler Sebring convertible. "Did you trade it?"

"Yeah, I know," he said, pulling a faux lecherous grin. "I gave the Sebring away. I'll explain when we get in," he added.

In the front foyer Ro unbuckled her gun belt and said, "I'll be right back." She didn't need to explain she was going to deposit the gun in her father's gun vault, to which she had her own key, downstairs in his den. A strong mindfulness for firearms safety was just one of the things her father had taught her.

By the time she got to the dining room that looked out a picture window across their backyard toward a wooded grove beyond, her mother had changed into a shirt and Capri pants, and her dad was setting small bowls of salsa and guacamole — both freshly made, of course — around a big tray of tortilla chips. The room was filled with a spicy aroma.

Out of deference to his wife, Big Red had loaded the stereo with several CD mixes of her preferred 60s and 70s rock artists... Simon and Garfunkel, The Beatles, Elton John, Eric Clapton, late Everly Brothers and Bonnie Raitt.

"What's everyone drinking?" Kate asked, heading toward the refrigerator. "We've got margaritas, beer, iced tea, and diet soda," she said.

"A margarita now, then iced tea with dinner," Ro said. "I'm on duty later."

"Beer," was all Mike had to say, since his first and generally only choice was a Killian's Red.

"Mar-ga-ree-ta," Tuck intoned, emphasizing each syllable.

While Kate got the drinks, Mike checked the oven. "The beef enchiladas and cheese and onion enchiladas should be ready in about ten minutes." Then, raising his eyebrows with a mock triumphant look, added, "And sopapillas for dessert," knowing full well they were a family favorite.

As they took their seats at the table and started scooping salsa and guacamole with the chips, Ro said, "Okay, Tuck, tell me about the car."

"Well, it gets a little complicated. You know Marty's Car Corner out on Main Street?" Everyone nodded. "They're an existing account I inherited from my predecessor. Once a month I go there with a crew and we tape Marty doing commercials of his weekly specials. Anyway, I saw the Miata on his lot and kind of fell in love with it."

"Oh, it's definitely *you*," Kate said, bringing nods of agreement from the others.

"Now, I gotta back up. The station was having a special

promotion in June. If you landed a new advertiser you got a special bonus on top of your regular commission. The bonus was ten percent of what the account contracted for. Well, in June I got the big Toro dealer, Horning's, out in Aldridge to sign-up for a two year, nearly sixty-thousand dollar campaign."

Quickly doing the mental math, Ro said, "Whoa."

"I know," Tuck agreed. "So I took the bonus and used it as the down payment on the Miata, and because it was a third of what they were asking, Marty gave me ninety days same as cash for the rest. I figure I can pay it off by the end of the summer."

Ever the practical one, Kate asked, "But what'll you do with it in the winter?"

"I'm thinking about leasing a four-wheel drive Escape in the fall. I'll garage the Miata; maybe just get it out once in a while on really nice days."

"Escape? Isn't that kind of *square* for you?" Ro said, trying to give "square" as deprecating an inference as she could, referencing both the car's shape and image.

"Sort of…. But it *does* come in this funky lime green."

"Of course it does," Ro said, rolling her eyes.

"Anyway, I gave the Sebring to the Boys and Girls Club to sell, like you did with all those Barbie sets."

When Ro had moved into her own apartment not quite two years ago and was cleaning out her bedroom closet, the question came up of what to do with nearly a dozen unopened Barbie dolls and accessory sets. Extracting a solemn promise it was to be their family secret, especially from her sister-in-law, Eileen, Kate suggested they be donated to the Boys and Girls Club either to be used or sold.

Out of the corner of her eye Ro caught Mike making an exaggerated face of innocence, looking up at the ceiling like he knew something she didn't.

Turning to her father, she said, "What?" Then, catching Tuck and her mother exchange a similar look, repeated, but with an overtone of suspicion, "Whaaaat?"

"Patrick will probably be moving out sometime next year," Kate said.

Ever since graduating from the University of Northern Iowa in June a year ago and landing his job with KLEE soon after, he'd been living at home in his old room.

"You're NOT getting married?" Ro said, then quickly added, shaking her head emphatically. "No, not that! Maybe moving in with somebody…"

"Neither. I'm getting my own place."

"Really, like an apartment? A house?"

"Again, neither." Then, turning to his mother, said, "It's really Mom's idea."

"Oh, thanks," Kate said with mock dismay. "Like I'm throwing you out on the street or something." Then, turning to her daughter, she said, "You know the tall Basso Brothers Moving and Storage building downtown near the river?"

"The one with all the windows?"

"Yep. The Bassos built a new warehouse out on the edge of town. Developers bought the old building and are converting it to loft apartments. We're," Ro knew her mother meant Kate Delahanty Design, "doing the common areas. Anyway, I thought it would be the kind of place Patrick would like." Out of the corner of her eye Ro saw her brother give a thumbs-up sign of agreement. "So I gave them an earnest money check. He's number one on the list; he'll have his pick of the units when they're done next year."

"I'll bet views of the river will be really cool," Ro said.

"I *know*," Tuck agreed with an expectant grin.

Pushing his chair back, Mike said, "I suspect dinner's ready. Who wants what?"

After filling their plates, taking their first bites and, as always, complimenting Big Mike on his cooking prowess, Mike turned to his son, adopted an ersatz look of disapproval, and said, "Enough with the Patrick this and Patrick that. This is *supposed* to be your sister's evening, you know."

Tuck hung his head in feigned shame.

Kate got everyone's attention with a sigh, then added, "I'm like Patrick. Up here," she touched her temple, "I *get* that you're my daughter sitting at my dinner table like you've done thousands of times over the years. And I *get* that we've all known you wanted to be a police officer since you were ten years old. But, it's still just a little disconcerting to see you *actually* sitting there in uniform."

Leaning forward conspiratorially, Ro said, first looking at her mother, then glancing around, "You know what's *really* weird? I *should* feel, I don't know, proud I guess, like I've finally made this great accomplishment. But," she added, gesturing to her uniform and lightly touching her badge, "it's almost anticlimactic. It just feels like…." She paused, searching for the right word. "*Inevitable*, like this was always *supposed* to be."

"It *was*, honey," Big Mike said.

"Ro, you know I don't take life very seriously," Tuck said, looking at his sister. "I always figured you took it serious enough for both of us. But this is me being serious for a change…. I sell *TV commercials*," he said, with more than a little disparagement. "Commercials for stuff people probably don't need or necessarily want, let alone can afford. If there is some kind of pecking order of important jobs in the universe, mine's gotta be near the bottom. But I'm good at it, I enjoy it, so it's what I do. I date lots of girls, mostly empty-headed gigglers. But I like them and they like me, so that's what we do."

But then he added, with what was for him uncharacteristic candor, "Sis, don't you get it? The *only* reason *we* can go about our day-to-day lives and do what we do is because there are people like you standing between us and chaos." Then, flashing his famous charming grin, he added, in an effort to lighten the moment, "I wish just once I could meet a girl like you, who knows who she is and has a purpose. Heck, I'd probably marry her."

"Oh, *r-i-g-h-t,*" Ro said with disbelief, rolling her eyes. "I've got twenty bucks that says you're still a bachelor when you're thirty." And then laughing, added, "Anyway, somebody like me'd scare the hell out of you."

"Probably. But at least I'd respect her."

Mike looked across the table at his wife, widening his eyes and raising his right eyebrow ever so slightly, as if to say, "Hey, we didn't do too badly with these two."

Kate smiled back at him and nodded briefly, silently agreeing.

"Who's ready for sopapillas?" Mike asked, also sensing the need to lighten things a little.

CHAPTER FOUR
DON'T MAKE THINGS HARDER THAN THEY NEED TO BE

Wednesday, July 9, 2003, early morning

Even though it was a pleasant summer evening around seventy degrees, with light winds, Bruce Battisen—Armstrong Two-Two—still had the black and white's windows rolled up tight and the air conditioner going. Ro hated it. To her it was like riding in a steel and glass bubble, completely cutoff from the world "out there" they were supposed to be in touch *with*, not insulated *from*. But it was Battisen's car and Battisen's watch, so she kept her peace…at least for the time being.

It was not quite 1:30 in the morning. Battisen was a week from his retirement and Ro was a week from the end of her five-day "orientation" rides with him. They'd been crisscrossing the southwest corner of the county, turning up this county road then turning down another county road, gradually working their way northward.

In Fort Armstrong County there were always at least three deputies on duty for every shift, like tonight. Sometimes there were as many as four; for instance, on weekends, when there was more likely to be trouble, or when there was some special event, like the county fair. The county was divided into three patrol sections, roughly the western third, the middle third, and the eastern third, with one deputy primarily assigned to each. Battisen's, and soon to be Ro's, patrol area was the western section, the ruggedest part of the county, with lots of hills and gullies.

Ro had so far spent the first two-and-a-half hours of their shift in the patrol car's passenger seat rubber-necking, looking in every direction. While she had driven on a few of the roads in the past, like the river road, Iowa Rt. 20, most of the roads were unfamiliar and she was fascinated by what she was seeing.

A farmstead with an old-fashioned, multi-story house surrounded by outbuildings and a silo or two, usually illuminated by a bright, pole-mounted security light....

A shadowy grove of trees hunkered in what looked like a valley, maybe with a shallow creek at the bottom....

A sprawling ranch house and attached garage plunked down on a half-acre of park-like grass next to the highway, usually with one or two spindly trees in the front yard....

Sensuously rolling fields of low beans or tall corn....

A cluster of dark buildings that sold feed or bought grain, or both, maybe with a dozen or so houses that constituted a tiny unincorporated town....

As they drove, Battisen occasionally offered information or advice....

Early in the shift they were westbound on Iowa Rt. 20, a four-lane road paralleling the Mississippi River, and were passing an interchange with the Illowa Freeway that was in the county, but close to Lee's Landing western city limits. Battisen jerked his head toward the on-ramp. "I hardly ever hit the freeway; I let the fourth deputy worry about nabbing the speeders or grabbing the illegals."

Ro cringed, although hid it, at the thinly disguised racial slur.

As the county's third shift dispatcher for nearly two years, Ro was well aware the fourth deputy on duty, whatever shift, traditionally patrolled throughout the county, but mainly concentrated on the busy Interstate 82 that ran east and west through the county, and the north-south Illowa Freeway that connected to I-82.

Later, when they were on an east-west stretch of paved road that for about two-plus miles was as straight as a string and as flat a board, Battisen told her, "This part of Fairly Road is real popular with the drag racers from Aldridge."

Later still, when they were on Two-Mile Road, a north-south gravel road near the county's western border, Battisen grinned and pointed to the left side of the road. "The farmer over there isn't too conscientious about keeping up his fences, so we get a lot of 10-54 calls" — *livestock on the highway* — "along here."

But more often than not it was Ro who sought information with questions.

As they were passing through a cluster of a several dozen houses grouped around a pair of churches and one tavern, she asked, "This is Fourth, right?"

Having studied the large county map on the wall in the dispatcher's office, Ro knew there were many small, unincorporated communities plunked down on the landscape for which the sheriff's department represented their law enforcement source.

"Yeah. I love that name, Fourth," Battisen said with a chuckle. "Supposedly it was the fourth place where the original settlers back in the eighteen-hundreds had tried to establish a town, after not doing too well in New York, Ohio, and Indiana."

When they were on Iowa Rt. 20, several miles further out into the county from the Illowa Freeway, they passed what looked like a sprawling pole building on the river side of the highway. Even at one o'clock in the morning on a Wednesday the parking lot in front was more than half full of mostly pick-ups and motorcycles. It had a tall, brightly colored cowboy hat motif sign next to the road: Corky's. It was well known both as a popular country-western bar and as a rough place.

Jerking his head toward the bar as they passed, Battisen said, "One thing I sure won't miss are the 10-B calls there."

"We haven't had any of those for a while," Ro said.

"And I sure as hell hope we don't over the next five days," Battisen answered.

In the not quite two years she'd been a dispatcher, Ro had perhaps a dozen times put out the call "Armstrong Two-Two"— *Battisen*— "10-10 at Corky's" —*fight in progress*— "backup 10-78" —*backup en route*— "10-B" —*fight involves Big Foot.*

At near six feet-seven and well over three-hundred pounds, Big Foot was a local legend. In another life he might have gone to college and ended up a beefy lineman for the Packers or Bears. But in this one he helped hump freight cars in the sprawling Sardee Railroad Yards several miles to the west, and liked to hang out at Corky's when he wasn't working.

"10-B" was a unique ten-code Fort Armstrong dispatchers had made-up years ago to warn deputies Big Foot was involved in a fight, but without having to say his name over the air, and was definitely intended to mean "wait for backup before going in."

Later they were headed east on County Road P which was really an extension into the county of Crosstown Road, Lee's Landing's major east-west commercial thoroughfare. Ro turned to face Battisen. "Another question?" he anticipated, sounding more amused than annoyed.

"Yep. Do we always drive the speed limit?" she asked, being careful to use an "I'm just looking for information" collective "we," meaning deputies in general, rather than what could be interpreted as a more accusatory "why do *you* always drive the speed limit?" spin.

"Always," he said. Then turning, his jowly face with a kind of long-suffering, fatherly expression, added, "Deputy, our job is to patrol our area and respond to any calls. You don't wanna make things harder than they need to be."

Ro had to bite her tongue to keep from asking the obvious follow-up question. "Why not slow down a little so you can really look around and see what's happening?"

They passed a brown local attraction sign that read, Shadowbrook Bike Path Trailhead, with an arrow pointing to a parking lot on the right. Ro had ended more than a few of her runs in the parking lot. They were just over two miles west of her apartment that literally sat on the western city limits of Lee's Landing.

A half-mile further Battisen pointed to the digital clock on the car's dashboard. It read 2:40. Signaling a left turn, he swung the car northbound onto County V. "We'll head up to The King for lunch," he said.

Ro knew, of course, he was talking about the sprawling Truck King gas station, restaurant, and convenience store next to the Interstate 82-Old Post Road interchange. As a dispatcher she'd heard the "10-7 The King" call — *out of service for lunch at the Truck King* — literally hundreds of times. The King was not only popular with Fort Armstrong County deputies, but state police and Lee's Landing cops as well, even though it was a couple of miles outside of the latter's jurisdiction.

CHAPTER FIVE
LUNCH AT THE KING

Wednesday, July 9, 2003, 2:45 a.m.

Ironically, Ro had never been inside the Truck King truck stop. She'd passed it many times on I-82 going to or coming from someplace or another, but never actually stopped.

Like all of its kind, it sprawled over something like four acres when you counted the sea of concrete where cars and campers and big motor homes and semi tractors and trailers parked. And like its kind, there was a nearly block-long center building with a tall red roof that housed the gas station, drivers' showers and dayroom, a convenience store, and a 24/7/365 restaurant. Three fifteen-foot tall, bright yellow, fan-like porticos, this time of night brightly illuminated from within, invited entrance to each section.

Battisen guided the patrol car down a central aisle between row after row of parking, and then swung it into an empty spot on the front row, right across from the entrance to the restaurant. It was one of more than a half-dozen spots labeled with a sign, "Police Vehicles Only." There were four other vehicles already parked in the row.

Another Fort Armstrong deputy's black and white Crown

Vic with 23 on the rear fender occupied one of the spaces…
Mel Schreiber's car. Which meant her friend Matero was the
"swing man" tonight. The sheriff department's policy said not
all deputies could be on lunch break at the same time, which for
third shift deputies was at 2:45, so the tradition was one deputy
did a "swing" through the entire county while the others took
their lunch break. Everyone took turns being the "swing man."

There was another Crown Vic, but this one was a cream white
and had "Iowa State Police" in block letters across the doors and
5-37 between the back window and rear windscreen.

And then there were two all black Chevy Impalas with
a splashy gold decal across the doors that said "Police," and a
smaller "City of Lee's Landing" in white block letters below.

At first Ro was mildly annoyed at what seemed to be the
privileged parking status for cops, but then rationalized, *Well, I
guess sometimes we might need to get going in hurry.…*

She was a little surprised by how busy the restaurant was
for what most people would think of as "the dead hour." A big,
u-shaped sit-down counter separated the convenience store
section from the main part of the restaurant; there were five
eaters at the counter. Two were clad in biker leathers, the other
three dressed casually, like tired travelers needing a break from
a boring nighttime drive. Six or seven of the maybe three dozen
four-person restaurant tables were occupied, including several
couples and even two families with children. Two waitresses,
one young, the other more like middle-aged, but both wearing
red Truck King-logo polo shirts and short black aprons, hurried
among the tables.

Knowing piped music would be unavoidable Ro was at least
glad it was country-western and not rock.

Just beyond the u-shaped counter were three long, eight-
person tables. Two had signs in the middle, "Drivers Only."
There were a half-dozen drivers between the two tables, some

talking, others just eating alone.

The third table's sign said "Police Only," where four officers were already seated. Ro didn't recognize the two Lee's Landing cops in their all black uniforms, or the state trooper, a sergeant, in his all khaki uniform.

She did know Deputy Mel Schreiber, called "Cueball," or "Cue" for short, because he shaved his head. On the force for eight years, Schreiber was a corporal. At five-seven he was the shortest deputy on the force, but compensated by being a workout buff, right down to having his uniform shirt tailored to emphasize his broad shoulders and narrow waist.

As they approached the table Battisen called out, "Hey, guys, this is Deputy Delahanty." Ro was grateful he didn't use her first name. "She's gonna be taking over for me next week."

Then, turning to Ro, Battisen said, "The statey," which was the nickname they used for state police, "over there is George Costas. The two Landing boys are Foley," he indicated the younger one on the right, "and Liggett," pointing to the one on the left. "And you know Cue," he added.

Cue, Foley, and Liggett had been involved in some kind of conversation. Cue glanced her way and waved a hand of acknowledgement, while Foley and Liggett just nodded. They then returned to whatever it was they had been talking about.

Costas, who was directly across the table, stood up, offered his hand, and said, "Deputy, good meeting you."

"Sergeant," Ro said, giving him a brief but firm handshake.

Battisen walked around the table to sit down at the end, between Schreiber on one side and Liggett and Foley on the other, leaving Ro and Costas standing, facing one another.

Costas, who looked to be in his late-thirties and had the long nose and kind of chiseled chin his Greek name would suggest, flashed Ro a slightly bewildered grin, shrugged and sat down, nodding for her to sit across from him, although with a raised eyebrow, which made it more like a friendly invitation than a command. As they sat, Costas said, "They're discussing"—he put air quotes around *discussing*— "whether the Cubs will pull an August crash, like usual."

Ro knew the much-maligned Chicago team was doing unusually well this year. She recalled Tuck mentioning something about them being in the lead in the National League's North Central Division, several games ahead of his favored St. Louis Cardinals.

Suddenly Ro was back in high school at a lunchroom table with her cousin Justin and Tuck and a bunch of his friends. They always seemed to be jabbering about something Ro knew little or nothing about—or more likely didn't really care about—or laughing about something Ro didn't find particularly funny, pretty much taking no notice of her and Justin.

Then Costas saved the moment when he said with a wry grin, "Now, I don't think the Cubs are gonna lose it; their new *quarterback's* gonna be great."

Ro laughed, for a moment dropping her "cop face." *Someone who doesn't take sports too seriously*, she thought with approval. "My brother's a big Cardinals fan, so I hear a lot about 'those darn Cubs,'" she said.

"My son's a diehard Cubs fan, you gotta be diehard to be a Cubs fan, so I get 'the rotten' Cardinals stuff," Costas said, trying to make conversation.

Just then the forty-something waitress, her plastic name tag said she was Karenlea, appeared, balancing three plates on one arm, and carrying a fourth in her other hand. She set the fourth down in front of Costas. "Here you go, honey," she said. It looked like a chopped steak with mashed potatoes and green beans, a roll, and coffee. She put what looked like a Cobb salad and a glass of iced tea in front of Schreiber, saying, "Cue." Then, glancing over said, "Hey, Bats. I'll get you and your new partner's orders in a sec'," as she gave Foley what appeared to be a cheeseburger, fries, and a milk shake, and Liggett another chopped steak plate.

Must be tonight's special, Ro thought.

She was a bit perplexed — well, more like miffed — over exactly how to feel about a waitress familiarly using a deputy's handle when it was a definite no-no for non-deputy department personnel to do so. She didn't blame Karenlea; after all, it was her job to be all friendly efficiency. But, just the same....

Suddenly the woman was standing beside Ro, her perfume noticeably strong. "Hi, I'm Karenlea, Deputy...," she glanced own at Ro's name badge, "...Delahanty. You takin' over for Bats...?" Except it really wasn't a question.

"Riding with him this week, on my own next week," Ro said.

"Cool," Karenlea said.

As she started to give Ro a menu, Ro held up her hand. "I'll have two eggs over medium, two sausage patties, hash browns, dry wheat toast, and black tea."

"Ahh, somebody who knows what she likes...my kinda people," Karenlea said with an approving nod.

Throughout the meal Costas and Ro chatted, him sharing he'd been a Mason City cop for nearly nine years before switching to the state police, Ro sharing she was new as a deputy but had been a dispatcher for the department for nearly two years. They were pretty much being ignored, and they in turn pretty much ignored the other four.

But then she overheard Liggett say something about "...the Gilbert PD is hiring." He was talking about the town of Gilbert, located adjacent to Lee's Landing on the east; at thirty-five thousand population, it was about a third the size of its neighbor.

Then Bats said in a voice loud enough for everyone at the table to hear, "You *do* know the difference between a Cub Scout pack and the Gilbert PD?"

To which Liggett, Foley, and Cue all chimed-in, in unison,

"Cub Scouts have adult supervision." And they all laughed heartily.

Ro hated that joke. She'd probably been on the job as a dispatcher no more than a couple of weeks the first time she'd heard it, and had heard it repeated many times since, sometimes about the Gilbert PD, but just as often about the Grand Island PD or Stephenson PD, the local departments in Illinois on the other side of the river. It was beyond her ken how one department could disparage another department, when, to her, all cops were brothers in blue, deserving of mutual respect and loyalty, no questions asked.

When Karenlea returned to refill coffee cups, Foley, who looked to be maybe in his early-twenties and seemed more than a little aware of his good looks, gestured toward the young waitress serving another table. "Hey, Karenlea, who's the new cutey there with the nice little ass? She could *refill* my coffee cup anytime." Obviously giving "refill" a double meaning.

Costas sighed audibly and rolled his eyes.

Karenlea, without missing a beat, continued to refill the coffee cups, but when she got to Foley poised the still half full and steaming pot in front of his face and directly over his crotch, tipping it menacingly. He pulled back with faux mortification.

"Foley," she said, smiling, except the smile didn't quite reach her eyes, "I'm kind of like the mother hen around here at night, so you might want to think of her like *my own daughter*." Then, leaning in to get right in his face, she added, "So, if I ever catch you sniffing around that young lady…,well, I've got lots of trucker friends who know where to dump the body parts *so they'll never be found!*"

Cue laughed. "Hey, Foley, you do *not* want to mess with Karenlea."

And Liggett added, "Jeez, I'd sure hate to slap cuffs on a fellow officer for chasing jail bait."

45

That's when Ro decided she very much liked Karenlea, but *didn't* much like the overgrown boy's club lunch that The King seemed to be.

Costas pushed his chair back. "Be safe," he said to Ro as he got up, dropping a five-dollar bill on the table.

"You, too."

Foley, Liggett, and Cue also pushed their chairs back and each dropped a five-dollar bill next to their plates.

At least they're decent tippers, Ro thought.

When they were gone, Bats picked up his coffee cup and moved to the empty seat next to Ro. "We'll get going in a sec', soon's I finish my coffee."

"Okay," Ro said, then asked, "When does Karenlea bring our checks?"

Looking slightly taken aback, Bats said, "She doesn't. We never get checks here. But we always leave Karenlea a good tip."

"Oh," Ro said, a little lamely, because for all intents and purposes she was speechless. She turned and picked-up her still half full cup of tea, not because she wanted more tea, but to hide her frown of shock.

Jesus Christ, free meals! Makes you wonder what the hell might be going on in the back room here we're not supposed to see, she thought.

Setting the cup down and pushing her chair back, she said to Bats, "I'm gonna hit the head. Meet you at the car."

"Sure," he said back.

As Ro threaded her way toward the restrooms over in the convenience store section, she took a short side trip to catch up with Karenlea, handing her a $20 bill. "That's for my meal and the rest is yours."

At first Karenlea looked like she wanted to protest, but then thought better of it. "Thanks, Deputy," she said.

Chapter Six
Raccoon Hollow

Friday, July 11, 2003, 4:20 a.m.

They were travelling west on Bell's Lake Road, a two-lane blacktop that wound its way through the thick timber and occasional sloughs alongside the wide and sluggish Pincatauwee River—known locally simply as "the Pinky"—that was Fort Armstrong County's northern border. They were nearing the end of their week together.

Ro twisted in her seat to take a longer look to the right, at something they were passing.

With a kind of patient smile, Battisen asked, "And what did you think you saw this time?" Throughout the week Ro had been rubber-necking—Battisen always drove—taking a longer look at things alongside the road.

"I was just noticing the nearly collapsed shed maybe twenty yards off the road," she said.

"I've seen it too...," Battisen said with more than a hint of forbearance.

"Well, the building's almost completely collapsed; clearly it's not good for anything. So, I was wondering why the driveway leading up to it is clear of weeds, like it's being used regularly?"

"Dunno. Maybe somebody just parks a tractor there?"

Or maybe someone's hiding drugs there, she thought, but instead said, "Could be." Then, shrugging mentally, thought to herself, *Heck, maybe you* are *making things harder than they need to be.*

They were headed for Bell's Lake, a small town of maybe a hundred or so homes on the Pinky River that, like many small towns either couldn't afford or didn't want to pay for a local constable, relied on the sheriff's department for police protection.

Earlier in the week Battisen had commented to Ro he tried to pass through Bell's Lake a couple of times a week. It had been yet another occasion she'd bitten her tongue. *What's wrong with at least once a* night? she'd wanted to ask, but didn't, thinking, *Seeing a sheriff's car more than a couple times a week might reassure the folks of Bell's Lake just a little.*

What's more, the comment had triggered a suspicion Ro had also kept to herself, but nonetheless had confirmed by watching and noting throughout the week; Battisen had a more or less regular pattern for driving through his section of the county. He almost totally stuck to the main paved county roads, rarely driving down one of the gravel roads that were still part of the county system. And he also tended to hit certain spots on certain days and at roughly the same time. All of which was, of course, entirely contrary to basic police procedure; you never wanted the bad guys to be able to predict where you might be at any given time.

Bell's Lake certainly hadn't made much of an effort zoning-wise. There were a few substantial houses, clearly decades old, scattered here and there. But between them were lots of small bungalows and a noticeable number of trailer homes, often with several vehicles, some clearly junkers, parked in front or to one side.

The main street, really just a continuation of Bell's Lake Road, looked across a muddy beach at what was known as Bell's Lake, essentially just an extra wide spot in the Pinky River popular with the local fishing crowd since the 1920s. There was a small grocery store and gas station, an adjacent bar and grill, and a bait and tackle shop that passed for downtown Bell's Lake, all still closed. But the town *was* waking up. Ro could see people climbing into their cars, or more likely pickups, probably heading off for a job in or near Lee's Landing on the other side of the county. There were more than a couple of guys putting coolers or tackles in flat bottom Jon boats on trailers behind their trucks, clearly getting ready to go fishing on the river.

Ro knew better than to ask, but couldn't help herself. "Do you ever stop and talk to these folks, you know, to get acquainted?"

Battisen frowned, but didn't take his eyes off the road. "Nah. Why would I do *that*?"

Ro knew it was a rhetorical question, he really didn't want an answer. *Why, indeed?* she thought.

As they had done on their last visit to Bell's Lake, on the western edge of town they turned left, south, onto County Road O to head up the bluff and out of the wide Pinky Valley. Maybe a quarter mile outside of town, before reaching the base of the bluff, they rolled past a gravel road off to the right, disappearing into what looked like a series of shadowy groves.

Ro remembered seeing the stubby little road on the big county map in the dispatcher's office, and that it was called Raccoon Hollow Road. Jerking her thumb toward it as they passed, she asked, "Do you ever patrol down there?"

"Down Raccoon Hollow Road?" Battisen said, shaking his head slowly. "Nah. It's a really rough old gravel road. You *don't* wanna go down there…. Nothin' to see anyway."

He had almost done a good job of sounding casual, except his "you *don't* wanna go down there…" had a kind of hard edge to it, like there was more to it than just a rutty gravel road. Of course, Ro knew, but didn't say aloud, *You don't wanna go down there. Don't bet on it.*

At the top of the bluff they emerged onto the county's rolling farm fields, dotted with bright pole lights stretching off into the distance, each indicating a farmstead. They turned right, west, and onto Upper Bluff Road, a two-lane blacktop that ran almost the full northern width of the county.

Behind them the sun was just peeking over the horizon, the eastern sky a mix of pinkish gray clouds, overhead a slowly brightening pale blue.

CHAPTER SEVEN
STREAKER

Sunday, July 13, 2003, 2:15 a.m.

"These are the kind of nights I always liked," Battisen said, "nice and quiet."

It was Ro's last evening of orientation rides in Armstrong Two-Two, and, not coincidentally, also Battisen's last night before his retirement. And he was right…it had, indeed, been a very "quiet" night: no speeders, no accidents, no bar fights, no domestic disturbance calls, no stick-ups.

"You'll be on your own come Tuesday," he said with a kind of "I wonder if you really know what you're getting yourself into" tone. On Tuesday afternoon Ro was scheduled to pick-up her squad car—she would be Armstrong One-Nine—and begin her own patrols of the western part of Fort Armstrong County at eleven that night.

"That I will," she said, trying not to let her excitement show too much.

"You know what I think the hardest part of retiring's gonna be?" he asked, but then answered his own question. "Getting my clock turned around so I can go to bed at night and be up

51

during the day. Hell, I'll probably end up driving my wife nuts," he chuckled.

They were eastbound on Upper Bluff Road, coming up on Peacock, a town of roughly twelve-hundred in mid-county. Unlike their previous four nights together, Battisen seemed in a more talkative mood, perhaps because he was so near the end of his twenty-plus year career as a deputy.

Ro started to say, "Does she?" But then her mouth dropped open and Battisen exclaimed, "Holy shit!" and hit the brakes. The patrol car screeched to a stop.

Some sixty or seventy yards ahead a naked man had suddenly emerged from the brightly lit gas pump lanes of the Quick Shop convenience store on the west edge of town. He quickly glanced over his shoulder in their direction, then turned and started running full tilt away from them, back toward town. They could see him clearly thanks to the car's headlights and a full moon halfway down the sky behind them.

Just then the radio crackled, "Armstrong Two-Two."

Ro picked-up the microphone, "Two-Two."

"Two-Two, we have a report of…um…. A, uh, possible 10-14" —*prowler*— "at the Quick Shop on the west side of Peacock," the dispatcher said; it was Gwen Teague, Ro's replacement as third shift dispatcher.

"10-04 Fort Armstrong," Ro acknowledged. Glancing at Battisen, she said, "Um, we know. We are 10-60" —*in the vicinity*— "and have the, uh, '10-14' in sight." She said "10-14" as if it had quotes around it.

"10-04 Two-Two," Teague acknowledged.

With an exasperated sigh, Battisen muttered, "A streaker, just what I frickin'need! I guess we better go chase this guy down before he scares the hell out of some poor old maid in town."

Battisen reached down and flicked on the car's red-blue strobe light bar, but when his finger went toward the switch for

52

the siren, Ro said, "Do you really think we need that? It doesn't look to me as if this guy is an *armed* threat or anything. Where would he hide it?"

"Very funny," Battisen said, and began accelerating in pursuit of their "10-14."

Just as they were passing the convenience store the streaker turned right, down a side street between some houses forty or fifty yards ahead of them, and they lost sight of him. When they turned onto the side street he had disappeared.

"Damn," grumbled Battisen, "he's probably hidin' behind somebody's garage by now."

Ro tried to slowly and carefully survey the area, hoping to spot some sign of their quarry; a furtive movement, a shadow that seemed out of place, bushes still disturbed from where he'd pushed through: Nothing.

No, wait…there was an open area about half a block up on their left that looked like a school yard of some kind and Ro caught a brief flash of white running across a football or soccer field.

Pointing to the field, she said, "Pull over there," trying to not make it sound too much like an order.

When the car stopped, Ro started to climb out, but Battisen said, "Wait a sec', gotta radio in." Rolling his eyes, he added, "Tell 'em we're gonna be on a damn foot chase." Except for Battisen the "foot chase" only lasted about thirty yards before he was bent over gasping for breath. "I'll go back and get the car," he panted. "Meet you on the other side of the school."

Ro, who was already ten yards ahead, called back, "Okay, I got it."

Turning back, she stopped as she could no longer see the streaker. She looked to her right and then her left. He'd only been about halfway across the open fields, so she was sure he couldn't have made it all the way to the other end so quickly, which meant he'd probably ducked into a woodsy area bordering the field on the right.

Staying five or six yards out, Ro started walking slowly along the edge of the woods, shining her bright LED flashlight into the dense stand of trees, but all she saw were thick gray tree trunks, shadowy shrubbery, and once in a while the glint of a night critter's eyes looking back at her, and all she heard was a chorus of crickets. While she was fairly sure the streaker wasn't a threat, she nonetheless kept her left hand down by her holster just in case she was wrong and he unexpectedly rushed her with a tree branch or something.

Almost to the end of the woods — there was a gravel road with a row of houses on the other side — her light suddenly caught a face and two raised hands in the woods, but they were low, as if he was in a sitting or crouching position.

"I give up!" the face said, its eyes wide with alarm.

Stepping a bit closer, Ro couldn't help but smile. "You seem to be in quite a predicament there, my friend."

"Uh, yeah," the guy said, glancing around with a look that said, "Isn't it obvious?" Maybe in his early-twenties, he was in fact naked, although Ro could only see his upper chest, raised arms and face, he was indeed sitting....

Sitting in the midst of a patch of thorny brambles.

As a hiker and trail runner, Ro was all too familiar with the nasty briers that liked nothing better than to ensnare the unwary and scratch the daylights out of their legs. Except, because he was *sitting* among the nasty things, Ro didn't want to think about all the spots on his lower body, perhaps some quite sensitive spots, which might have been ripped by the sharp spines.

"I'm Deputy Delahanty," she said, trying to sound both casual and authoritative at the same time. "You gotta a name?"

"Brent.... Brent Tuttle," he answered, clearly embarrassed.

"Well, Mr. Tuttle, my partner should be along with the patrol

54

car any second on the road over there," she gestured to her left. "*He* can get you a blanket and help get you out of there," she said, putting a slight emphasis on "he."

While Ro knew she was supposed to keep things professional, the situation was so bizarre she couldn't help herself, and asked, "Mr. Tuttle, why in the world are you running around Peacock without your clothes?" Then she added, suspiciously, "Have you been drinking?"

"Well, yes," he answered, dropping his eyes and hanging his head. "And why I'm naked is a really embarrassing story."

"Oh, I'm sure it *is*," Ro said. Just then the patrol car crunched to a stop on the gravel road. As she heard the car door open she turned and called to Battisen, who was just climbing out, "I've got our, uh...uh..."—he wasn't really a perpetrator, or a suspect, or a prowler—"*subject* kind of in custody, but he needs a blanket for cover, and some help."

Battisen retrieved a rust colored fleece blanket from the patrol car's trunk and trudged over.

"Ouch," he said, looking down at Tuttle, trying hard to suppress a grin.

"I'll, uh, go over by the patrol car while you help Mr. Tuttle here get out of his... *predicament*," Ro said.

"No, I think we better call in some more back-up," Battisen said, no longer able to hide a chuckle. "This guy looks pretty dangerous to me."

"You *aren't* gonna give us any trouble, now, are you Mr. Tuttle?" Ro asked.

"No, ma...." He started to say "ma'am," but quickly corrected himself, "No, *deputy*."

"Okay. You know, it really doesn't look very good on our report if we have to shoot a naked man."

Spreading out the blanket, Battisen started toward Tuttle, cussing under his breath as his trousers kept getting snagged by the thorns. After a moment Battisen had the young man at the patrol car and gingerly helped him into the backseat; he had not cuffed him. While the blanket did cover most of Tuttle's nakedness, his legs and feet were clearly covered with dozens of scratches, some of them still oozing blood.

"Am I under arrest?" Tuttle sheepishly asked Ro, who was standing next to Battisen.

Glancing at Battisen for confirmation, she said, "Not yet. Why don't you take a minute to tell us how got yourself into this mess?"

"Well, it was supposed to be a prank on our friend's fiancée, but something went wrong. We were at his bachelor party earlier, and yes, we'd had a *few* drinks. Anyway, when the party broke up several of us were in a car on the way home and we got this bright idea, well, maybe not so bright, for one of us to show up naked at the convenience store where Kathy, our friend's fiancée, works; you know, just to get a rise out of her."

"Did you just make a bad pun Mr. Tuttle?" Ro asked, working hard to suppress a grin. "You know, we can throw the book at you for that."

The young man just stared back, confused; apparently his "pun" had not been intended.

"You're not talking about Kathy Wells, are you?" Battisen said, addressing Tuttle.

"Yeah, that's her," Tuttle said. "She works at the Quick Shop in Peacock. All I was supposed to do was walk up to the front windows to where she could see me, wave, and then get out. My guys were gonna pick me up with my clothes a few hundred feet down the road. Except it sure *wasn't* Kathy in that convenience store, so I panicked and ran...."

Shaking his head, Battisen said, "What went wrong, Mr. Tuttle, is you morons went to the *wrong* convenience store.... You went to the Quick *Shop*. I know Kathy, she works at the Kwik-

Stop," he said, emphasizing "stop." "It's over on the east side of town. I get coffee there all the time."

"Oh," Tuttle said with disbelief. "There're *two* convenience stores in Peacock?"

"Yes, there are, and you picked the wrong one," Battisen said.

Hanging his head, Tuttle said, "Look, I know you guys probably have to take me in, but I'm really embarrassed about this. Could we go back so I can at least apologize to that lady I freaked out, tell her I'm sorry."

"You stay put," Ro said to Tuttle, more like a request than an order, "while I talk to my partner for a minute."

Leading Battisen a few yards away, she said, "How about this…we take him to the hospital to get those cuts looked at. Meanwhile, he can use one of our cell phones to call his friends to pick him up there with his clothes. We write him a ticket for DO," which meant disorderly conduct, a misdemeanor, "and let it go at that. I don't get the feeling he's really a pervert who'll be out running around exposing himself just for the heck of it." An indecent exposure charge was *not* a misdemeanor.

Glancing at his watch, Battisen sighed. "Deputy, in just a few hours this is gonna be *your* beat, so you call it."

"Okay. Oh, and we *will* stop by the Quick *Shop* so Mr. Tuttle can make his apology."

After they'd dropped Tuttle off at the hospital in Lee's Landing, leaving him with his citation and in the company of his friends who'd brought his clothes, they climbed back into the patrol car. Ro was trying to figure out how to say thanks to Battisen for a good idea. Most of what she'd "learned" from him during their orientation week she thought of as lessons on how *not* to be a good cop, which, of course, she wouldn't share…and she was pretty sure he had not intentionally meant to give her any advice…. And, finally, while she liked to think she probably would have figured this out on her own anyway, she thought the practice of getting to know the people who staffed all-night convenience stores on her patrol route was a good one, as you never know what they might be able to tell you. So she just decided to keep it general....

"Corporal," she told Battisen, "in case I don't get to say it later, I sure appreciate you spending your last week as a deputy with me; it's been a real honor."

During most of the week when he'd talked to Ro he'd kept his eyes on the road, but now he turned and nodded. "Well, thank you Deputy. I think you're gonna be a *good* cop; the department's lucky to have you."

"Thanks," Ro said, not knowing what else to say.

"By the way," Battisen added, "they're throwing a little retirement get together for me at Lefty's." Lefty's was a bar in Lee's Landing started by the former sheriff, Lefty Struve, after he'd retired. It was, of course, popular with law enforcement types. "A week from Friday night. I hope you can stop by."

"You bet," Ro said, pretty sure she didn't really mean it.

CHAPTER EIGHT
FRANK REYNER

Sunday, July 13, 2003, 6:30 a.m.

TC's started life back in the 50s as a classic country service station, with gas pumps out front, a small office, and two service bays. It sat a mile east of the intersection of County Line Road and Iowa Rt. 20 in the far southwestern corner of Fort Armstrong County, just outside the main entrance to Five Falls State Park. Over the years, though, it had adapted to changing economics. The service bays had been replaced with shelves of basic food items, snacks, and sundries, and coolers filled with milk, pop, water, sports drinks, and beer. A healthy portion of TC's business was from Five Falls' campers who always seemed to find they needed something. A lean-to-like addition was added to accommodate a snack area, with small plastic booths, a microwave, coffee and cappuccino machines, wrapped sandwiches, and fresh pastries.

Both Fort Armstrong County and the State of Iowa had running tabs with TC's, so it was a popular spot for state and county workers, deputies, state police and state employees to fill-up their official vehicles.

Battisen pulled into one of the gas islands on the far left and started filling the Crown Vic's tank, while Ro went to the office to sign for the gas. She had just started back toward the patrol car when a new Dodge Ram pickup rolled to a stop two islands over. It was clearly an Iowa Department of Natural Resources (DNR) vehicle; forest green paint job, small yellow warning strobe in the middle of the cab roof, State of Iowa decal on the door, and Park Ranger in two-inch high, white block letters under the cab window.

"Hmm," Ro muttered to herself, "new ranger gets a new truck."

Ro and her family were well-acquainted with the beat-up, decade-old pickup Bill Cummins, the Five Falls park ranger for as long as Ro could remember, had driven; the Delahanty's had been picnicking and camping at Five Falls State Park since she was a child. As a teenager, she'd gotten hooked on running on the state park's and adjacent county forest preserve's nature trails.

The Ram's driver's side door swung open and a thirty-something male clad in the forest green uniform of a park ranger slid out, his badge and sidearm visible even from thirty feet away. The sidearm looked like a revolver, which kind of surprised Ro, as she didn't think any law enforcement agencies were still using six-shooters. He paused, seemed to watch Ro for a moment, then smiled and waved. What Ro had expected she wasn't sure, but what came next was not it. Rather than turning to start gassing his vehicle, he instead strode across the concrete driveway separating them with his hand outstretched.

"Hello, Deputy," he said. It was a genuine, open "hello," not a formal "I'm acknowledging you" hello. "I'm Frank…Frank Reyner," he pronounced his name "rainer," like it was a verb, "the new park ranger," he added, nodding toward the state park's entrance behind him on the other side of the highway.

He was just a smidge taller than Ro, perhaps five eleven, and slender. His sandy hair was cut in a butch and he was clean shaven. His face was narrow, with a full mouth and straight brows. He was not wearing a hat, so she could clearly see his dark eyes under the bright overhead lights. Indeed, his eyes were his most striking feature…intense, but friendly. And they seemed to be laughing, not a superior at-something laugh, but a genuine "I'm really enjoying meeting you" kind of chuckle.

All her life Ro had been pretty good at reading body language, sometimes seeing subtle things that revealed a great deal about someone, often way more than they would have liked to disclose. Indeed, this stranger's body language, the way he strode across the pavement, but not in a hurry, the way he held his head high, with confidence, but not arrogance, exuded friendliness.

Ro took his offered hand. It was a firm, respectful handshake, definitely not an "I've gotta prove something" crusher, or a perfunctory "let's get this over with" shake. And there was something more; she had an instant, but strong sense, of openness and warmth about the man.

"Nice to meet you, Ranger, I'm Ro Delahanty," she said, instantly kicking herself mentally for using her first name instead of a more professional "*Deputy* Delahanty." There was something engaging about Frank Reyner that made that kind of informality not only possible, but entirely comfortable.

A fleeting frown passed across Reyner's brow, like he was trying to think of something he'd forgotten, but then dismissed it.

"When did you get here?" she asked, again mildly chiding herself, *What's with this small talk?* She knew Cummins had been promoted to an area supervisor and had moved to Cedar Rapids, some hundred miles away.

"Just moved in yesterday," Reyner said. "Well, at least I *unloaded* the boxes from the U-Haul. Most of them are still sitting in the garage waiting to be moved to their assigned rooms and get unpacked."

The singular "I" and "me" pronouns, Ro noted. *No wife, no girlfriend.* Then, grumpily added to herself, *Why should* you *care if he's got a wife or girlfriend?* Except she found she did seem to.... And then she even had to somewhat crossly squelch an urge to offer to help him with his unpacking: That's how she'd met her first serious boyfriend, helping him move into the house next door to hers in Lee's Landing. While that relationship had been more than grand and had ended reasonably well, it had nonetheless ended.

What's going on here? she scolded herself. *I don't even know this guy. He could be a secret S&M fiend or something,* she thought, then laughed at herself for how ridiculous that sounded. But, while she didn't want to admit it, even tried to resist acknowledging it, there *was* something quite genuine—it was the only word she could think of—about this Frank Reyner.

Battisen, who had finished topping off the patrol car's tank, returned the nozzle to its spot on the pump, crossed behind the patrol car, and held out his hand. "Ah, you must be Cummins' replacement, the new ranger."

Reyner did a brief double-take, glancing from Ro to Battisen and back again. He was clearly a little bewildered, but whether it was because he was confused by two deputies or because he didn't want to stop talking to Ro wasn't entirely clear.

"Well, I don't know about *replacement,*" he finally said, turning to Battisen. "I understand Cummins was quite well-respected around here. But, yes, I *am* the new park ranger. Frank Reyner," he said, extending his hand to Battisen, raising one eye brow as if to gently ask, "And you are?"

"Deputy Battisen," Battisen said, giving Reyner's hand a brief shake. "In fact, very soon," looking at his watch, he added with a grin, "like in about half-a-hour, I'll be *retired* Deputy Battisen." Gesturing toward Ro, he said, "Deputy Delahanty will be taking over this part of the county from me." Turning to her, he added, "We need to get going."

As she was climbing into the passenger side of the black and white, Reyner said to Ro, "Well, then perhaps I'll be seeing you again, Deputy." With most guys who said something like that it would feel like being hit on, but with Reyner there wasn't a trace. Ro found she liked it.

"Might," Ro answered. She knew it was lame, but couldn't think of anything else to say.

As Battisen was turning right onto Rt. 20 to head toward Lee's Landing and the sheriff's department headquarters, *and* his retirement, Ro glanced behind her and caught a glimpse of Reyner standing in the middle of the gas-up lane watching them drive away.

"Seemed like a nice fella," Battisen said, his eyes on the road ahead.

"Yeah, I guess," Ro answered, trying to sound as casual as possible, but at the same time wondering what the hell had just happened back at TC's. Reyner had in no way come-on to her, at least not in any of the overt ways most guys tried. Yet there was no doubt in her mind even in their brief—what, maybe six or seven minute?—encounter he'd clearly been attracted to her, although she could not imagine what she could possibly have done to in any way affect that.

CHAPTER NINE
ARMSTRONG ONE-NINE 10-8 — IN SERVICE

Tuesday, July 15, 2003, 3:30 p.m.

Corporal Eddy Rivera swung his Crown Vic patrol car into the parking lot of Ro's apartment complex where she was waiting in uniform. It was near the end of his day shift and he was going to ferry her to the county garage so she could pick-up her own patrol car, Armstrong One-Nine, for her first solo patrol shift starting later in the evening.

A deputy for six years, Rivera had become friends with Ro when she was a dispatcher. He had the smoldering good looks of his Puerto Rican heritage

"Hey, Ro," he said as she slid into the front passenger side. It was a sunny, low 80s afternoon with a slight breeze; she was grateful he had the car's windows open.

"Hey, Eddy," she said. "Thanks for the lift."

Rivera's deputy's handle was "Slats," left over from his point guard days for Hubbard High School in Lee's Landing, but Ro just automatically used the name by which she knew her friend.

"No problem," he said, turning right onto Old Post Road, heading toward downtown and the sheriff's headquarters.

"Gloria wants to know if you can come over for dinner on the twenty-seventh; it's two weeks from last Sunday, around one. I'm barbecuing," he added, knowing Ro always seemed to like what he cooked. Ro's work schedule was Tuesday through Saturday, so she could take a morning nap after her Saturday shift. It was a schedule they'd often done before.

"Love to," Ro said.

Gloria was Gloria Olin, Rivera's live-in girlfriend of several years. They had a small bungalow in an older part of Lee's Landing. Eddie, Gloria, and Ro each took turns hosting dinners once a month or so. Eddie and Gloria's dinners were generally much more elaborate than Ro's, which tended to favor one dish casseroles, or just good old takeout.

After several seconds of silence in which Ro stared straight ahead out the patrol car's windshield, Rivera said, "Okay, so what's on your mind? I know that look, and it says something's buggin' you."

Ro turned toward her friend. "When you're on patrol, do you always drive the speed limit?"

He glanced over at Ro with a frown, like he didn't really understand the question, or more specifically what the *real* question behind it was.

"When we were on patrol last week, I noticed Bats always drove exactly the speed limit and always kept his eyes pretty much on the road ahead."

"Did you ask him about it?" Rivera said.

"Yeah.... He told me our job was to patrol our area, to respond to calls, and not to look for trouble."

"And *you* think?"

"That it *is* our damn job to look for trouble!" she said, with a more vehemence than she'd intended, but at the same time finally letting a week's worth of frustration out for some air.

Rivera burst out laughing, then realizing it might be taken

the wrong way quickly added, "I'm not laughing at you, I'm laughing at...at...." Turning to her, he said, "God, I hope that old fart didn't screw you up too much with more bad advice like that." Then, changing tone, said, "Ro, *you're* right; it absolutely *is* our job to look for trouble. It is what the hell they pay us for!" Then he added, "And no, I don't always drive the speed limit."

"You sometimes go slower so you can just look around and *see* stuff."

"Of course," he said with a frown, as if there weren't any other logical answer.

Suddenly signaling a right turn, he pulled into a supermarket's sprawling parking lot and swung the car into a space near the street, far from the shoppers' cars. Shifting in his seat toward Ro, he said, "There's only one piece of advice you need about being a cop, Ro. *Pay attention to your instincts...*always! If your instincts tell you to go slow through some area and look, then that's what you do.

"You've been through the academy just like the rest of us. You're even working on your degree in LE," law enforcement, "which is more than most deputies can say," he said. "And yes, we should always take advantage of all the training we can get. But what makes a really good cop, a cop that can go into harm's way and come out the other end, is good instincts. Do you know why I started talking to you when you were a dispatcher and why we became friends?"

Ro shook her head.

"Because every time I saw you in the dispatcher's room, if you weren't on a call you were studying the big county map on the wall. For cryin' out loud, you were trying to *memorize* the damn thing. Every other dispatcher was either flirting with a deputy or just staring off into space. Then, when I found out you wanted to be a deputy, well, I just knew you'd make a good cop," he said. Sort of embarrassed by the turn the conversation had taken, he pointed to her and said with a laugh, "And you know I'm not just blowin' smoke up your ass to get into your pants. I've already got Gloria."

Ro laughed too. "I know, and she'd unman you with a dull knife if you ever tried."

"Oh, I have no doubt," he chuckled.

"So, I'll just take it as a compliment."

"Good, 'cause that's how I meant it."

***

Wrench, although his birth name was Steve the chief mechanic for the sheriff's department was always known simply as Wrench, led Ro out across the floor of the cavernous garage to where six patrol cars were lined up. Five of them were either hiked up on jacks with tires missing or had their hoods open.

But the one on the end was clean, shiny, and said "ready to go."

Wrench stopped in front of the car, extended his arm, and said, "Deputy, meet One-Nine. You're lucky…One-Nine's one of our newer cars, only thirty-eight thousand miles."

Reaching into the pocket of his coveralls, he withdrew a ring with a remote fob and several keys and handed it to Ro. "Here you go," he said. As Ro took the keys, he started to walk away, but then turned back and added with a grin, "Take care of my baby."

"I will," Ro answered.

The car looked exactly like all cop black and whites. But to Ro it was beautiful: *It was hers.*

The front fenders and hood and the back fenders and trunk lid were black. The top was white, with a low profile light bar stretched across the middle, and the doors were white. Across the front door it said Fort Armstrong County in three-inch high black block letters, and then Sheriff in tall, thin letters below. On the back door was a decal of the department's five-pointed star badge, and on the dark rear fender it said 19 in white block letters.

Ro stepped close to the patrol car and ran her hand across the smooth white top, stopping to touch the light bar. "Hello, One-Nine," she murmured. Then, looking around quickly to make sure Wrench was out of earshot, said under her breath, "Hello, Mr. Pete."

It was probably inevitable; the squad car was black and white, just like Peter Panda, and they were both important to her in their unique ways.

Ro walked slowly around the car, just looking, lightly running her hand over the curves of the hood, the roof, the trunk lid. She thought of what she was doing as kind of making the car her own, so was startled when Wrench returned and said, a little defensively, "We already checked. No dings or dents."

"What?" Ro said, suddenly noticing him. "I...I wasn't looking for dents...," she stammered, frowning. "No...I wasn't implying you guys weren't doing your job. I was...." She paused, trying to think of what to say, then decided something close to the truth was the best approach. "Hey, you know, this *is* my very first squad car, so I was just getting acquainted."

Wrench grinned, he understood "getting acquainted," and said, "You know, some of the guys even have a nickname for their car."

Oh my god, did he hear me? Ro said to herself, having thought giving her car a name was, if not unprofessional, certainly too "girly."

"They do?"

"Yeah, they'll roll in here and tell me, 'Betsy here needs an oil change,' or 'Big...,'" he started to say something, then, with a flush, said, "Well, anyway, I'd bet a maybe a quarter of the deputies have some kind of nickname for their cars."

"Really?" Ro said, feeling better about having already given her car a name, but not quite ready to admit it.

Opening the driver's side door she slid onto the bench seat, closed the door and gave Wrench a salute. She discovered the seat was just right for her long legs; she could reach the pedals easily, but the steering wheel was just at fingertip distance. Reaching down beside the seat, she found a small lever, released it, and leaned forward. The back rest snapped forward just a hair and she could now comfortably wrap her hand around the steering wheel.

The inside of the car looked exactly like every other patrol car looked; the usual instruments on the dashboard, a steering wheel and turn signal-windshield wiper control wand, headlight switches, radiator and air conditioning knobs. But there was also the microphone and its spiral umbilical; there was the bracket on the dashboard to hold a radar gun; there was the Mobile Data Terminal (MDT) mounted on a pedestal over the center hump; there was the series of switches just below the computer terminal controlling the siren and light bar; and, of course, there was the ugly steel mesh barrier to make sure someone placed in the back seat stayed in the back seat.

To Ro it was all magnificent.

Snapping on her seat belt, she turned the key and the car's powerful 4.6-liter V-8 engine rumbled smoothly. Putting the car into gear, she rolled slowly out of the big garage doors, stopped at the end of the driveway to slip on her aviator-style sunglasses, then, signaling her turn, went left on Third Street, which would take her west for several blocks to intersect with Old Post Road and back to her apartment.

All the windows were down and she had her elbow resting out of the left open window. It was exactly like she'd always imagined it would be. Looking around, front, right, left, rearview side mirrors; front, right, left, rearview side mirrors; front, right.... Looking at the cars, at a big SUV here, at a pickup there, a delivery truck on her left.... Row after row of storefronts lining both sides of the street, with their garish signs near the curb, cars pulling into or out of their parking lots....

Front, right, left, rearview side mirrors; front, right, left, rearview side mirrors; front, right....

Without really thinking about it, Ro lifted the radio microphone from its bracket on the dashboard, pressed the transmit button, and said, "Armstrong One-Nine."

There was a just the briefest of pauses before the radio crackled back, "Armstrong One-Nine go." Ro recognized dayside dispatcher Sandy Freers' slightly nasal voice acknowledging her call, but there was also a hint of unspoken confusion in her tone, like, "What are you doing on the air now, you're not on duty until tonight?"

"Armstrong One-Nine, 10-8" — *in service* — Ro said simply into the microphone.

Again, there was just a brief second of silence. Then Sandy's voice responded, but this time with a tone of totally routine professionalism, as if she finally got what Ro was doing, like they had done this a thousand times before: "Armstrong One-Nine 10-04" — *acknowledged*.

Armstrong One-Nine, in service. Acknowledged.

And that's when Ro lost it.

There was no prelude, no slow tearing up. Suddenly she was gasping and sobbing, the tears unbidden, cascading down her cheeks, pooling along the bottoms of her sunglasses.

Armstrong One-Nine, in service. Acknowledged.

Confused and embarrassed, she yanked off the sunglasses and tossed them on the passenger seat. She tried wiping the tears with the back of her uniform sleeve, the completely incongruous and ill-timed thought, *Thank heaven I don't wear mascara,* passing through her mind.

Not quite knowing what to do, but knowing she couldn't stay on a busy street, she flipped the turn signal for a right turn and swung the car into the parking lot of a long strip mall, with a bunch of specialty shops, insurance offices, and chiropractors. Pulling into a parking spot that faced the street, away from other cars, she thought, *Maybe they'll think I'm watching for speeders*, yet at the same time knowing how silly an idea it was because she was still in Lee's Landing, not her regular jurisdiction.

Gripping the steering wheel with both hands, Ro fought to get herself under control, but lost.

Armstrong One-Nine, in service. Acknowledged.

Yes, she'd been sworn in…. Yes, she'd put on her uniform…. Yes, she'd holstered her big, powerful handgun…. Yes, she'd known at an intellectual level for several months she was *going* to be a cop, ever since Mark Ballard had sent her an official letter offering a deputy's position.

Armstrong One-Nine, in service. Acknowledged.

Yes, she'd been a wannabe since she was in fifth grade.

But somehow that simple radio exchange…

Armstrong One-Nine, in service. Acknowledged.

…captured, and at the same time set free, everything that had been important to Ro Delahanty for half her life. And it was just overwhelming…. It was no longer a *someday*…no longer a *not quite yet*…no longer a *soon*…. She was behind the wheel of *her* black and white Ford Crown Vic Police Interceptor patrol car!

Ro blinked and tried to deny the tears. *Cops don't cry.*

But then Eddy's words echoed in her mind. *Pay attention to your instincts.* And she understood this was something she needed to do at this moment; that it was her way of accepting….

Armstrong One-Nine, in service. Acknowledged.

…that the Ro Delahanty she had been no longer existed, that that Ro Delahanty had been replaced by a new person. Not by a pod person, that thought brought a wan smile, but by *Fort Armstrong County Deputy Sheriff Ro Delahanty*. It was *real* now!

Still holding the steering wheel, looking out the windshield at nothing and at everything, she let the tears flow. It felt good.

Chapter Ten
Front, Right, Left, Rearview Side Mirrors...

Tuesday, July 15, 2003, late evening
and Wednesday, July 16, 2003, early morning

"Good evening, Mr. Pete," Ro said, sliding behind the wheel of the patrol car. "Let's go help protect the world from the bad guys." It would become her regular nightly greeting.

She knew she was supposed to be excited. After all, this was her first official solo patrol as a deputy sheriff...being "out there" in possible harm's way. Of course, she knew cops truly being in harm's way was very rare; it was one of the things her police academy instructors had stressed. "Ninety-nine point nine percent of your time will be routine," they'd said, "which should be the way you *want* it."

Certainly she had some feelings of anticipation about what she would see and feel and experience tonight. But as she settled into the driver's seat and for just a few seconds sat there, she nodded, because what she was mostly feeling was a sense of inevitability, like she was finally where she belonged.

Ro had backed the car into a spot under a streetlamp in a far corner of the parking lot outside her apartment in the Westwynd complex, where she could see it from her front room but not where other cars tended to park. She didn't want her patrol car dinged by some careless parker.

After donning her uniform a few minutes ago, she had carried Peter Panda from his spot in her bedroom down the hall to the big sliding glass door in her living room that looked across the parking lot. Holding him up to see, she said, "Well, there's your namesake, Peter: I call him Mr. Pete in your honor. What do you think?" After a pause, she agreed, "Oh, yes, I think he's beautiful too."

Now turning the key and firing up the Crown Vic's V-8, she first turned on the headlights and then logged-in on the unit's Mobile Data Terminal (MDT). Touching the "Log-in" icon on the MDT's screen, she entered her password; most deputies, she knew, used their name or their birth date, which wasn't very secure. Instead, Ro'd chosen the combination to her locker in elementary school: 23-6-44. Although the sheriff's department computer now had her officially on duty, the dispatcher's monitor at the department headquarters showed Armstrong One-Nine "in service," many deputies still observed the tradition of radioing in, even though it wasn't at all necessary.

Picking up the mic from its bracket on the dashboard, she said, "Armstrong One-Nine."

"One-Nine go," came Gwen Teague's baritone acknowledgement.

"One-Nine 10-41" — *beginning tour of duty.*

"10-04 One-Nine."

The MDT also told Ro her GPS position, the weather — it was going to be in the 60s, clear, with light winds — and had a heads-up message board that had replaced the deputy's beginning of shift briefing down at headquarters. There'd been a bank robbery in Grinnell, halfway across the state, earlier in the afternoon, and the perps had reportedly been seen heading east on I-82 in a dark gray van, although by now they'd be well past the Lee's Landing area if they'd stayed on the interstate. An elderly man had wandered away from a nursing home in Gilbert. There'd been an anonymous tip about a high school beer party at a private residence near Pleasant Hill off County Road Q, which wasn't in Ro's patrol area. The U.S. Department of Homeland Security's terrorist threat level was low.

As this was the first time she was using the patrol car at night, she found the instrument illumination dial on the lower left side of the dashboard and experimented with it until the dashboard's instrument lights were as dim as she could make them and yet still read their information. She wanted to preserve her night vision for seeing outside of the car.

Similarly, it took a few minutes of exploration before she was able to drill down in the MDT's set-up menu and find the setting allowing her to dim the screen's brightness to just twenty percent; it had originally been set to a distractingly high seventy percent.

Ro's patrol area was roughly the western third of Fort Armstrong County, stretching from the Mississippi River on the south to the Pincatauwee River on the north, from roughly the western city limits of Lee's Landing on the east to the Makuakeeta County line on the west. It was about three times as long north to south as it was wide east to west. And it was also the most rugged part of the county, with lots of hills and valleys, curvy farm fields interspersed with timbered pastures, and meandering creeks.

She had spent much of the evening in her study agonizing over how she would structure her patrol routes from night to night in order to avoid as much as possible any predictable patterns...trying *not* to emulate Deputy Battisen's example. She'd made several copies of a simplified county map and had experimented with ways to mark the maps with different colored highlighters for different days of her patrol, when it occurred to her that that in and of itself would amount to a pattern.

75

The only way you're not gonna have any patterns, she'd finally concluded, *is to be as random as you can.*

Which was why she'd decided she would just have to rely on her instincts — *instincts again* — and each evening decide which way to go based on however she felt.

And which was why from the Westwynd parking lot she turned left onto Old Post Road. Then, in half-a-mile, she turned left again onto Crosstown Road, which became County Road P outside the city limits and which would take her roughly into the mid-section of her patrol area.

It was a cool night for mid-July, with the moon just a couple of days past full. Still, Ro had all the windows of the patrol car open because she wanted to not only *see* her patrol route as she passed through it, but to hear it and even smell it.

Because County P was only two lanes, the posted speed limit was fifty-five, but she stayed at least ten miles an hour under that.

Front, right, left, rearview side mirrors; front, right, left, rearview side mirrors; front, right....

For some strange reason she recalled an incident when she was maybe nine or ten years old and had been going somewhere with her dad. They were on North Avenue, a mostly commercial thoroughfare in Lee's Landing, when her dad glanced up and said, "Oh, they changed the billboard." She had vaguely recalled it had been promoting a local car dealer, but now featured one of the nationally-franchised casual restaurant chains.

It was a street they'd driven along dozens of times before, and a billboard they'd probably "seen" an equal number of times, but somehow it stuck with her that even though her dad was completely familiar with the road, he'd noticed the changed sign. *Maybe he noticed the change* because *he was so familiar with the landscape,* she thought.

At least that was exactly how she hoped to learn her patrol area, to become so familiar with it any change would stand out.

76

While not all change necessarily meant trouble, she understood for a cop, things that seemed out of place meant stop and take a look, check it out — *instincts*.

Front, right, left, rearview side mirrors; front, right, left, rearview side mirrors; front, right….

A little more than halfway across her patrol area she turned right, northbound onto County Road B, then jogged over to County Road T, still northbound. At first she'd tried to concentrate on everything she was seeing….

A collection of metal barns and newer out buildings with three tall silos: Maybe a confined feeder operation?

A dark tree line with a lone tall dead tree that stood out, white and skeleton-like against the shadowy silhouette of the grove: A pasture, maybe with a few head of cattle down on their knees?

A weedy gravel drive seeming to meander off into nowhere: Maybe leading to an abandoned farmstead?

A ranch house near the road with all its lights on at 12:30 in the morning: An insomniac?

A pickup truck parked in the middle of a field some fifty yards off the road; maybe waiting for the return of a tractor in the morning?

And then there were the smells. The dry, musky smell of new mown hay and the rank, nostril pinching, but all too familiar stench of manure — the pig dung noticeably more pungent than the cow droppings — were to be expected.

But there was a section of road out in the middle of nowhere with an oddly perfumy scent; maybe a nearby, but unseen patch of clover, or perhaps someone had for some strange reason simply emptied a bottle of aftershave alongside the road.

And then there was a spot with the overpowering odor of burnt rubber, like someone had set a stack of old tires alight, so strong Ro pulled the patrol car over to the side of the road, got out, and carefully looked in all directions to see if she could spot a column of smoke or the flicker of flames. Nothing.

After a couple of hours it quickly became apparent to Ro it would be impossible for her to literally memorize every house and barn and silo and field and pasture and creek and gravel road and grove of trees and country church and small town.

Anyway, she thought, *Dad hadn't literally memorized North Avenue.*

So she began to *just look.... Front, right, left, rearview side mirrors; front, right, left, rearview side mirrors; front, right....* Seeing, but not really focusing. Familiarizing, but not trying to memorize.

CHAPTER ELEVEN
RACCOON HOLLOW, REVISITED

Wednesday, July 16, 2003, 2:12 a.m.

Ro turned north off Upper Bluff Road onto Forest Preserve
Road, which dropped over the bluff into the Pinky Valley and
led to the entrance of the county's Pincatauwee Forest Preserve,
which, as its name implied, butted up against the river. While the
forest preserve itself was not in her patrol area, Bell's Lake Road,
which headed west from the forest preserve's entrance, was. She
was thinking she'd spend twenty minutes or so patrolling Bell's
Lake, not only covering the main drag, but perhaps visiting some
of the side streets as well: there weren't that many.

With the near full moon and no clouds, while things were not
as bright as day, they were certainly brighter than most nights.
The thick stands of trees dominating the Pinky Valley even threw
distinct shadows.

Instead of passing through Bell's Lake at the posted limit of
twenty-five miles an hour or maybe even a bit faster, as Battisen
had done, Ro kept her speed at twenty or even a bit under. When
she got to the first cross street on the eastern edge of town, it was
called Gunderson, she signaled a left turn and took it past Second

Street then turned right onto Third Street, going west.

Like the main street, it was a collection of bungalows, many in need of paint, mobile homes, and a few more substantial homes. In the bright moonlight she could see some had gardens in side yards or pots of flowers on a front porch or deck. Most had at least two vehicles parked in front or on the side, usually a pickup and some kind of sedan or mini-van. And perhaps one out of four had a flat bottom boat on a trailer. The houses were all dark, except for a few porch lights.

Suddenly her headlights illuminated a figure walking along the left shoulder of the road; Bell's Lake did not have sidewalks. It was an old man, bald, but with a fringe of white hair above his ears and a closely cropped white beard. He was short and had an old man's belly. He looked for all the world like a gnome, but his walk was confident, certainly not an elderly shuffle. The big collie that had been romping just ahead of him stopped and stared curiously at the patrol car, its nose twitching, clearly not used to seeing a vehicle at this hour.

Rolling to a stop next to the old man, Ro said with as much pleasantness as she could, "Good evening, Sir."

"Good evening," he said, then, glancing down at the patrol car's door, added, "Deputy."

His voice was gravelly, and though pleasant, had just a shade of wariness.

"Nice night for a walk," Ro said.

"Well, Rufus there," he said, nodding toward the dog, "can't make it through the night like he used to." Then, cocking his head slightly as if he'd thought of something, added, "Where's the other deputy we sometimes see?"

"You mean Deputy Battisen. He's retired. I'm Deputy Delahanty, his replacement."

He grinned devilishly. "Delahanty, huh…. Well, I'm *Murphy*," he said, clearly enjoying their shared Irish heritage. "But what're you doing up here on this back street? Is there anything wrong?" he asked, glancing around, like maybe he'd missed something.

"No, there's nothing wrong, Mr. Murphy. Since I'm new to this section of the county I thought maybe I'd drive around a little, just to get more familiar."

"Murph," he said, "everyone calls me Murph. If you say Mr. Murphy around here they'll think you're talking about my father. He's ninety-six and still lives with me over there," gesturing with his left hand toward what was clearly a double-wide mobile home a little further along the street. Then he added with undisguised sarcasm, "Just driving around, huh? The other deputy usually went through here like a bat outta hell down on the main drag, and sure never came back *here*."

Ro almost said, "I know," but then bit her tongue, not wanting to criticize a deputy even though he might deserve it. Instead she changed the subject. "You and your dad fish a lot?"

"This year we are. The Pinky's up and there're fish worth catchin'. Last year the river was so shallow 'bout the only things in it were logs'n'frogs," he said with a laugh at his own joke.

"Goin' out today?"

"Yep. Dad'll be up in a couple of hours. I'll make us some breakfast and we'll be out at least for the morning."

"Well, good luck, Murph," Ro said. Then, raising her hand in a kind of a wave, put the patrol car in gear and let it start rolling forward.

"Take care, Deputy," Murph called after the car with a wave, then turned to the dog. "Come on, Rufus, let's get on home."

Bell's Lake's Third Street ended in another hundred yards at County Road O, where Ro turned left to head back up into the county. But in a quarter mile she saw Raccoon Hollow Road going off to her right.

You don't *wanna go down there.... Don't bet on it....*

Out of habit she hit her right turn signal, even though there

81

was no car in sight in either direction, and swung the patrol car onto the gravel road. Not sure what to expect, Ro backed off the gas pedal, creeping along at well under twenty, the car's tires crunching noisily on the gravel.

Within fifty yards she discovered two things. For one, Battisen had been right, Raccoon Hollow Road *was*, indeed, a rough road, with lots of potholes and wash boarding that jarred the car and its lone passenger. The other was that she seemed to have passed into an unusually dense stand of thickly grown trees, almost cave-like in its gloom. Even the wan silver light from the nearly full moon disappeared, leaving nothing but dark shadows and even darker murk.

Ro slowed to almost an idle speed crawl, looking around, front, right, left, rearview side mirrors. After another fifty yards or so the road curved gently off to the right and the thicket of trees thinned a little, but then swung back to the left. On the right was a twenty yard wide, weedy beach leading down to the Pinky River, silvery in the moonlight. Even if she couldn't have seen the river, she'd have known there was water nearby from the swampy smell. On her left were maybe a dozen cottages facing across the road toward the river; a few had porch lights on and a car or truck parked nearby, but most were dark. No one was outside, which probably shouldn't be surprising given the hour.

She wondered if anyone was awake and perhaps peeking out, unseen, from behind drawn curtains, curious about such a late night visitor noisily crunching along the gravel road. And then smiled to herself at what would undoubtedly be their surprise to see it was a sheriff's car.

They'd probably wonder who I was after, she thought, with a wry grin.

Reaching the end of the row of cottages, she was confused for a moment by what appeared to be a dark presence looming high above the road, but then the car's headlights revealed the steep side of a finger of the bluff thrusting toward the river. At first the road seemed to end at several thick posts with yellow reflectors, but then she saw it made a sharp left turn, disappearing into another shadowy thicket.

Even as the car, still moving at a walking crawl, entered the dark thicket, Ro knew something was not right. Battisen's words came back to her—*You* don't *wanna go down there*—and she remembered the trace of imperative in his voice.

The further she moved into the murky thicket the more palpable her discomfort seemed to become. It wasn't a physical discomfort, like a cramp in her leg or a crick in her back from riding too long. It was more like an amorphous anxious feeling, not yet focused enough to be a specific fear.

After thirty or so yards the road, now more like a pair of twin ruts, seemed to fork and she could see several shadowy buildings nestled in clearings among the trees. As the car moved forward it was clear the road didn't really fork, but rather was a big loop. She quickly counted eight homes around the loop, and was a bit surprised these weren't the typical weekend fishing shacks she'd expected, but were more like the kind of neat and tiny bungalows that dominated several older neighborhoods in Lee's Landing.

All were dark. No safety lights hung from poles or garage fronts. No glowing porch lights. No thin slivers of light peaking through drawn curtains. No flickering blue suggesting a TV still on.

As the patrol car's headlights swung across the yards she could see several had not recently seen the work of a lawn mower, and some were partially hidden behind a small copse of trees or unruly shrubs.

Ro was just making up her mind that at least this part of Raccoon Hollow was pretty much abandoned and she could skip it on any future patrols when quite unexpectedly the formless discomfort she'd been feeling bloomed into a palpable sense of fright. *You* don't *wanna go down there*...the menace in Battisen's warning now seemed even more explicit.

Suddenly she jerked back in her seat, quickly bringing the patrol car to a complete stop. Quietly opening the driver's side door, she slipped out and slowly looked all around, front, right, left, back, trying to locate where her sense of alarm was coming from. Was someone trying to sneak up on the car? Was there a hidden sniper? Maybe just a rabid coyote? Or a crazy drunk who'd think it was funny to scare the cop?

But she saw nothing; no surreptitious movements, just dark shadows and even darker gloom.

And then her instincts told her the peril she was feeling wasn't from an immediate threat, but rather seemed to have its source in some time long-forgotten, yet enduring, like something really dreadful had once happened in one of these houses.

Now sure there was no imminent danger she slid back into the patrol car, put it in gear and let it roll forward slowly, but persisted in her vigilance.... *Front, right, left, rearview side mirrors....*

Continuing around the loop and rejoining the entrance road past the cottages now on her right, she left the gloomy collection of houses behind, her sense of anxiety slowly dissolving. Ro sighed audibly, already beginning to discount her fears as just first patrol jitters in what was clearly one of the loneliest spots in Fort Armstrong County.

Turning right up County Road O, she glanced at her watch; 2:35, nearly lunch time. Picking up the microphone she hit the transmit button. "Armstrong One-Nine to Armstrong Two-Six, go to tac two."

Armstrong Two-Six was Rick Matero. Tac two was a channel allowing patrol cars to talk to one another without the entire county network listening in.

"Two-six," her radio squawked. It was Matero answering

her.

"Hi, Cowboy. I'll take swing man tonight," she said. She didn't add it was her intent to "take swing man" as often as she could get away with so as to avoid a repeat of the boy's club lunch that had made her so uncomfortable her fist night out with Battisen. She'd dodged that for their remaining four nights together with the excuse she had brought her lunch, a pretext Battisen had seemed to accept. But now she needed a new reason to avoid the lunches.

"Anyway, it'll give me a chance to get more familiar with the other parts of the county," she said into the radio, perhaps as much rationalizing to herself as she was justifying it to Matero.

"10-04," Matero acknowledged.

CHAPTER TWELVE
THE BOTTOMS

Monday, July 21, 2003, early morning

Ooo-OOO-woo-woo
Ooo-OOO-woo-woo

Ro didn't have to open her eyes and pick-up the cell phone on the night stand next to her bed to know it was around 5:30 a.m. Her friends the mourning doves, with their gentle cooing, were her regular natural alarm clock.

She'd grown up listening to the doves that lived in the grove behind her home. She loved their cheery morning greeting; it was one of her favorite childhood memories. The doves greeting her this morning lived in a slightly over hundred-acre area of ancient trees and wetlands behind her apartment and next to Shadowbrook Creek locals called The Bottoms. The birds had turned out to be a serendipitous bonus to the several other reasons she'd chosen this particular apartment in the Westwynd Complex not quite two years ago.

The Shadowbrook Bike Path running along the back of the Westwynd Complex in general, and through The Bottoms in particular, was one of her two favorite places to go for a run. The other was the complex of hiking-equestrian trails in Five Falls State Park and the county's adjacent Great River Forest Preserve, where she intended to go later in the morning.

The Shadowbrook Bike Path took its name from Shadowbrook Creek that it paralleled for some fifteen miles from out in the western part of the county, then traversing Lee's Landing and neighboring Gilbert before emptying into the Mississippi River. For much of its length it was a paved, ten-foot wide ribbon snaking its way through a wide swath of grass and trees bordered by residential neighborhoods, several parks, with their ball fields and picnic grounds, and the sprawling Meadows on Shadowbrook Golf Course on the east and the county's Long Hills Golf Course on the west.

The bike path was where she'd done most or her running since she'd started when she was in sixth grade. In those days the path had ended at the east edge of The Bottoms, which also happened to be the western city limits of Lee's Landing. After all, no city in its right mind would want to annex a useless chunk of land like The Bottoms, so it was "out in the county" by default.

The Bottoms was one of those curiosities of geography probably left over from a bygone glacier. It was a more or less shallow bowl butting up against Shadowbrook Creek on the south. The south side of the creek was a long rock face that in some spots jutted twenty feet above the creek. Several drainage ways emptied into The Bottoms from adjoining residential neighborhoods or farm fields on the north or west, turning it into a series of swampy swales interspersed with small hillocks of ancient sycamores, ash and cottonwoods; *and* a rare and regal American elm that had somehow escaped the ravages of Dutch elm disease.

In fact, she could see the regal elm from her second floor apartment, the top of which was just now catching the first morning rays of the sun. It reminded her of the great shagbark hickory that dominated the grove she could see from her childhood bedroom, a tree she'd loved climbing and always had a special affection for. Soon after moving into her apartment she'd explored The Bottoms and found a faint deer path through the thick underbrush allowing her to touch, or as she thought of it, "pay her respects," to the elm.

Several years ago Fort Armstrong County had put together some state and federal money and extended the bike path for just over two miles through The Bottoms on a series of wooden causeways and earthen berms, and then out past the Long Hills Golf Course to a trailhead on County Road P.

For Ro there was something really special about The Bottoms. She didn't tell anyone because she thought it might sound more than a little creepy, but she liked to think of it as her "green cathedral." Ironically, the reasons most runners shunned The Bottoms — the trail was crushed gravel, it was eerily quiet, it had a rich, earthy smell, and the stately trees arched over the path like a cathedral's soaring arches — were the very reasons Ro loved it.

The Bottoms was why, when Ro wanted to get her own place, the Westwynd Complex was her first, indeed, pretty much her *only* choice and its view of The Bottoms and the great elm was why she had chosen this particular building.

Ooo-OOO-woo-woo

Ooo-OOO-woo-woo

Rolling over from her usual sleeping position on her left side, Ro propped herself up on a pile of pillows against her headboard and smiled to herself, recalling how taken aback she'd once been when she'd mentioned to someone she liked the sound of the doves in the morning. They'd responded angrily, "I *hate* those *damn* things, waking me up when it's still dark! I'd shoot 'em if I could find 'em!"

She was naked; she'd been sleeping naked ever since she'd gotten her own place. Unwinding the flannel sheet she used as a cover from around her waist and between her legs—Ro tended to be a nighttime tosser and turner—she swung her legs out of the bed and padded into the bathroom down the hall to pee. Then she padded into the adjacent larger bedroom she used as her study and stood next to a battered reclining chair which had been positioned to look out of a sliding glass door at The Bottoms. She stood with her hands on her hips and legs slightly spread, gazing at the wall of trees turning golden green in the early morning sun.

She always figured it would take a mighty effort of slogging through lots of thorny underbrush and then scrambling up a tree to just exactly the right height, for a wannabe peeper to catch a glimpse of her nude, so she thought he deserved his cheap thrill.

The soft, cool morning breeze flowing through the open screen side of the sliding door caressed her, slightly stiffening her nipples and ruffling the hairs of her pubis. It was like a lover's touch, only instead of the insistent, needy touch of most human lovers, it was gentle and undemanding.

Ooo-OOO-woo-woo

Ooo-OOO-woo-woo

Ro closed her eyes. She loved the early morning sounds of The Bottoms….

The doves, continuing their conversation, were joined by lots of other chirps, tweets, and whistles from birds she couldn't identify. The trees sighed and whispered to her; not words a human might use, but rather expressions of feelings and energies, expansiveness and acceptance. It always made her feel at peace.

Because she worked nights five days a week, experiencing a sunrise this way was only a once or maybe twice a week gift. But, after a few minutes, Ro muttered to herself, "Okay, lady, time to get moving."

Going back to the bedroom, she picked up the T-shirt and cut-off sweats that always ended up on the floor next to her bed and slipped them on. Unfortunately, she needed to cover herself when moving around the front section of her apartment, where the living room and kitchen-dining areas were situated, because they looked out across a parking lot and main apartment complex drive at several other buildings, and she hated drawing the vertical blinds.

In the kitchen she peeled and sliced half a banana and some strawberries and threw them into her blender, then added a handful of blueberries, some yogurt, a dash of milk, a couple of tablespoons of whey protein, and a squirt of honey, and turned it into a thick, blue smoothie...her usual breakfast. Eggs over medium, a couple of sausage patties, hash browns, toast, and a mug of strong black tea—a taste she'd acquired from her father—would be her second breakfast later.

CHAPTER THIRTEEN
E-MAILS

Monday, July 21, 2003, early morning

It was still a little early for a run, so she padded down the hall to the study. She had deliberately chosen the larger of the apartment's two bedrooms for her study. Along one wall were several three-shelf bookcases, one packed with the textbooks for her online bachelors of criminal justice classes, while the other two were filled with medals and trophies from her years of judo and shooting competitions. In a prominent position on one bookcase was the newest trophy, an eight-inch wide by twelve-inch tall, thick slab of plastic with a 1911-style automatic pistol etched near the top. Below a bronze plate was engraved with four lines: "Ro Delahanty / Iowa's Best Shooter / U.S. Shooter's League Iowa State Champion / Iowa Sportsman's Club, Des Moines, Iowa, April 27, 2003."

Next to the bookcases, in the corner by the closet door, was her gun vault. In it were her deputy's service belt and Sig .357; a nine millimeter Glock 34 and quick-draw competition rig; her compact nine millimeter Glock 19 off-duty weapon and its paddle holster; a Ruger Mark II Government Competition Model .22 LR, the gun she'd learned to target shoot with, and with which she had won at least half of the trophies; a Browning BPS 12 gauge for skeet shooting; and a Stevens Model 311A .410 shotgun, the gift from her father with which she had first been introduced to shooting when she was ten years old.

Opposite was her desk and a couple of two-drawer filing cabinets, looked over from the wall above by more than two dozen mostly 8x10, and few 5x7, framed candid photographs of Ro's family, both immediate and extended, and her best friend, Atti Mehra. The latter showed a pair of fourteen-year olds grinning stupidly at the camera, their heads together. While Atti's Indian heritage was obvious from her large eyes and slightly chubby cheeks, that was the year she'd started streaking her spiked hair, having chosen lime green for the day the photo was taken. Ro was then still wearing her hair long, pulled back in a thick, bushy, brick-red pony tail.

There was one of Ro and her cousin Justin, except because they had pretty much grown up together they acted more like a brother and sister. It was when they had gone to their senior prom together; he because he was gay and still pretty much in the closet at the time, and she because no one had asked her, probably because she had sent plenty of "don't ask" signals. Justin looked very classy in a white dinner jacket and black tie, and she looked very sophisticated in a sleeveless, high-neck Kelly green floor-length evening gown. It was one of the very few times in her life Ro had actually enjoyed being in a dress.

There was even one of Sonny Colletta, her first serious boyfriend, now friend, taken just last spring at a press conference after he'd won the NCAA individual golf championship as a junior at Arizona State. Clearly a publicity shot of some kind, on the bottom was printed, although it tried to look as if it'd been handwritten, "Best Regards, Sonny Colletta." But it had been crossed through with a thick black marker, and up in the sky he'd jotted, "Ro… Thanks for being a great friend, Sonny."

Ro dropped into her office chair and turned on her laptop. Then she slid one of her CDs into the computer, this one featuring Beethoven's *Pathetique* piano sonata; the String Quartet No. 8 in E minor, one of the "Rasumovsky" quartets; and the *Kreutzer* violin sonata. Logging into her e-mail account, Ro smiled because there was one from Justin; no surprise there, as she got one from him pretty much weekly; one from Atti, who she heard from mostly weekly or every other; and, a little surprisingly, something from Sonny, who she only heard from once a month or so.

Sonny Colletta had been Ro's first lover; she would always treasure what she had learned about being a woman with him. But nearly three years ago he had headed off to become immersed in top-tier collegiate golf competition, she had started an associate's degree in law enforcement at Mississippi Valley Community College, over in Illinois, and the relationship had evolved into a good friendship.

Knowing she'd probably spend more time with Justin's and Atti's e-mails, Ro opened Sonny's first.

Unlike Atti's e-mails, which tended to be light and chatty, Sonny's tended to be sporadic; newsy, but not talkative. For instance, the subject line on Sonny's e-mail simply said, "Number One!" She also noticed he'd sent it to a long list of addresses, some of which she recognized as his family.

"You'll be reading about it in the paper in a few days," he wrote, "but I wanted to let you guys know first. The new AGA," which Ro knew meant the Amateur Golf Association, the amateur's prestigious counterpart to the Professional Golf Association (PGA), "ranking is going to have me at number one." Which Ro knew meant he was going to be ranked the top amateur golfer in the world. "Ain't that the coolest?"

Ro grinned. *You've gotta be in seventh heaven, my friend,* she thought. *You're a great golfer that thrives on the competition, but you also love the whole scene.* They had often talked about how, even as then just a high school level championship player, the other side of the golf world, besides the intense on-the-course competition, included loads of schmoozing with fans, with tournament sponsors and officials, and with the ever-present and adoring groupies.

"Would you believe next week I'm off to Japan?" he added. "I'll be playing in the Nippon Invitational outside Tokyo. More then. Love to everyone, Sonny!" *Typical Sonny,* Ro thought, *short and sweet.*

Ro clicked reply, and knowing everyone on the list would see it, typed, "Congratulations, Sonny! You know you've always been number one with us. Japan, huh? I bet if somebody sponsored a tournament on Mars, you'd be the first in line in your spacesuit. Best, Ro."

She hit send.

The subject line on Justin's e-mail said "New Job," which piqued Ro's curiosity. Justin was between his junior and senior year in UCLA's drama and theater program. If he'd said "New Role," that would have made more sense, because he was always getting a "new role" in a college production or some local theater gig; but Justin and a "job" didn't quite fit.

It turned out his "job" was going to be as a part-time reader of recorded books for a company called Listen-Up. He had auditioned for it, along with a bunch of others, and had been hired because of what the recruiter called "the amazing flexibility" of his voice, like being able to do many accents and even an acceptable female.

"They're going to start me off with a couple of shorter romance novels," he wrote. "You know, breathless bodice-rippers, to see how I do and how the listeners rate me. It'll be early next year before the first one is out...I'll let you know."

Ro's was grinning from ear to ear when she typed her reply.

"Well, this shouldn't be any surprise. After all, your first book reading was *The Cat in the Hat*; and if I recall you got a pretty enthusiastic response to that one."

When they'd been in a sixth-grade language arts class together, one project was to give a speech in front of the class. Justin had been very frightened of the prospect until Ro suggested they rent the appropriate costume and he do a dramatic reading of Dr. Seuss's *The Cat in the Hat* to the class. The costume had transformed him and he'd done a great job, getting the most applause by far of any of the speakers: And Justin was hooked, after that trying out for and mostly winning parts in every school production throughout middle and high school.

Atti had been in India with her parents visiting relatives for two weeks and would be there another two weeks. As Ro's best friend, Atti was the one person she had always been able to be completely open with, even more so than with her parents and brother. The subject line on her friend's e-mail was typical Atti, irreverent and a little enigmatic. "I'm The Invisible Woman." Although of Indian heritage, Atti was a thoroughly American Millennial, highly independent, suspicious of tradition, and impertinent. For the last week she'd been sharing her amusement, and sometimes frustration, at the cultural shock of being completely immersed in the highly traditional Indian culture. One of her earlier e-mails had been titled "Stranger in a Strange Land," and had been a riff on Robert A. Heinlein's classic sci-fi novel of the same name, in which she'd gone on about not being able to "grok" — which in Heinlein's novel meant to truly connect with — traditional Indian culture.

When Ro opened Atti's e-mail she found her friend had even located and embedded an illustration of a woman, but it was all just dots, so it looked indistinct, like the woman wasn't really there.

Shaking her head, Ro muttered to herself, "Nice touch, Atti."

"I finally got it," Atti's e-mail said. "Over here they want their women to be *present* to take care of the kids and to serve them, but to not really be seen and certainly not heard...to be the Invisible Woman. While I'm okay with the fact it's *their* traditional culture," she wrote, "sometimes it does tempt me to lift my T-shirt and flash my tits, just to see their reaction."

Oh, that would have been quite a show, Ro thought. Shorter and stockier than Ro, when Atti was sixteen she'd had her breasts "worked on," so would have been flashing a voluptuous set of 36 Ds at her undoubtedly stunned relatives.

Of course, it was Atti's usual impudence, so it was certainly no surprise, and part of Ro figured her friend was just trying to be funny and didn't really mean to go through with it.

In her answer Ro tried to reflect, at least a little, Atti's cheekiness. "So, do you need me to send you some more duct tape for that wicked mouth of yours?" Knowing how hard her friend was probably finding it to keep her assertive tongue in check. Ro closed by relating a couple of anecdotes about her "orientation" ride with Deputy Battisen, ending with, "Of course, I'd never tell him this, but I think of most of his advice as lessons on how *not* to be a good cop."

While Atti and Ro often teased one another, the teasing was never mean or judgmental; one of the hallmarks of their relationship was each accepted the other for who they were.

After sending off her response to Atti, Ro spent nearly an hour in her Management in Criminal Justice online class's discussion forum, making her own comments and responding to other's comments. After just a year in the local community college's criminal justice program, Ro had switched to the Parker National Institute of Criminal Justice's online program, and was now more than halfway toward her bachelors.

She and several of her classmates were in the midst of a debate about the pros and cons of Theory X management, which basically says employees are lazy and need to be forced to do their jobs, versus Theory Y management, which assumes people are self-motivated and *want* to do a good job.

One participant, who she knew from his student profile was a sergeant with the LAPD—she always pictured him as looking like Russell Crowe, who played a cop in one of her favorite movies, *L.A. Confidential*—had been arguing Theory X was the only way to manage people, especially in the quasi-military law enforcement environment.

"While I'm realistic enough to know there are lazy people who might need some kind of Theory X approach from time-to-time," Ro wrote in her response, "Theory X is essentially a negative approach that, if you apply it to everyone all the time, becomes a self-fulfilling prophecy. In other words, they will live *down* to that expectation."

Ro double-checked her entry. She'd learned her biggest issue was sometimes her brain got ahead of her fingers, and she had a propensity to leave out words, something Word's spelling and grammar checker wouldn't necessarily catch. Finding her comments okay, she hit the post command.

"Grrr," she said, in a half grunt, half expression of satisfaction, pushing away from the desk and stretching her arms high over her head, and sticking her legs straight out to get rid of the kinks of nearly ninety minutes hunched over the computer.

"Okay, now it's time for some fun," she said out loud to herself, which to her meant a nice long run.

CHAPTER FOURTEEN
NESHNALA

Monday, July 21, 2003, late morning

Going back to the bedroom, Ro made her bed, then pulled off her T-shirt and cut-off sweats and tossed them on the bed. Opening a dresser drawer, she got a pair of white cotton briefs and slipped them on, then pulled a dark blue sports bra over her head and down over her breasts. Standing in front of the mirror, she fitted her thumbs up under the bra just below each armpit and pulled the side of each breast back, in effect flattening herself under the bra for a more comfortable fit.

"Don't want any bouncy boobs, do we?" she told Peter Panda.

Over the panties she stepped into a pair of loose fitting dark blue running shorts and over the bra pulled on a dark blue T-shirt. For her feet were white cotton footies and Merrell Ascend Glove trail running shoes. Heftier than regular running shoes, they were built for the uneven and often obstacle strewn woodland trails she favored. The finishing touch was her "official" running hat, a battered Chicago Cubs cap, not because she was a Cubs fan, she wasn't any team's fan, but because it was a valued gift from Tuck. A big St. Louis Cardinals fan, her brother had gotten the hat as a joke in a Christmas white elephant gift exchange in high school and had given it to his sister.

Taking a dark leather fanny pack from its hook in the closet, she added her wallet and ID, keys, cell phone, and a granola bar to the front section, and her Glock 19 and an extra magazine, retrieved from the gun safe, to their elastic holding straps in the back section. A half-liter water bottle filled with orange flavored Gatorade would go in an elastic holder next to the pouch.

The drive from her apartment to Five Falls State Park and the adjoining Fort Armstrong County Great River Forest Preserve took only a few minutes. Between them they covered over two thousand acres in the southwest corner of the county. The state park portion included two large campgrounds and a boat launch on the Mississippi. Both featured scenic drives and picnic areas and between them more than fifteen miles of hiking and equestrian trails; over the years Ro had run on virtually every mile.

But the biggest attractions were in the state park.

A limestone outcropping had created a series of spectacular palisades facing the Mississippi River. Rock Creek, which began in Makuakeeta County to the west, but eventually meandered into Fort Armstrong County, had over the centuries cut a gap through the rocks, creating a series of waterfalls, some dropping nearly twenty feet, before emptying into the Mississippi. It was how the park had gotten its name.

On top of the bluff toward the back of the state park was Neshnala, a great white oak tree that, at an estimated two-hundred-and-fifty years, was believed to be one of the oldest living trees in Iowa. The tree had been called Neshnala by the Sauk Indians that lived in the area in the 1700s; modern translations said Neshnala meant "Tree of Knowledge."

Neshnala was accessible by a road off County Line Road, which bordered the state park on the west, and was a popular field trip for school children, families and Sunday drivers. Ro as a student, and Ro with her family, and Ro as an adult runner had probably visited Neshnala at least a hundred times over the years.

The main entrances to the state park and the forest preserve were below the bluff, off State Route 20. Neither park had a day use fee, so Ro simply waved to the attendant as she rolled by the registration and information booth several hundred feet from the state park's entrance.

As she passed a crossroad leading to one of the campgrounds on the left and to the ranger station some hundred yards to the right, she glanced in that direction, thinking she might see the green Dodge pickup. It wasn't there, or at least not where she could see it.

She felt a twinge of anticipation. *Maybe he's out and around in the park and I'll bump into him,* she thought. But then she second-guessed herself. *Hey, what do you care? You came here for a run, like you've done lots of times.*

Except, try as she might to dismiss the idea, she knew she *did* care, at least a little.

The main entrance road continued for another half-mile through thick forests, past another road leading to the second campground on her right. Then, as it neared the towering limestone palisades, it swung left and continued for another three-quarters of a mile to end in a large parking lot next to a small man-made lake at the base of the falls.

At not quite eight in the morning, there were only a couple of other cars in the lot.

Ro climbed out of the car, taking her keys but locking the fanny pack inside. She went around to the front of the car, near a picnic bench, and began what she thought of as her own version of a Tai Chi routine, which was, in fact, a series of muscle stretches to get ready for a run. With its slow repetitions and holds of various exercises, it took her a little under three minutes to complete.

Now ready to run, she returned to the car, retrieved the fanny pack with its bottle of Gatorade and clicked it on.

What was known as the Neshnala Loop Trail was a six-foot wide crushed gravel path beginning at the north side of the parking lot, but almost immediately turned into a series of switchbacks as it climbed up the face of the palisades next to the tumbling falls. At the top of the falls the trail became a loop of little over two-miles following Rock Creek to the north, then swung to the east through wooded glades and hollows before reaching the meadow where Neshnala stood. Then it curled back south and then west along the edge of the bluff, offering several spectacular overlooks of the Mississippi River and the Illinois shore beyond.

Most visitors found the climb up the switchbacks strenuous, with some even quitting, breathless, halfway up. For Ro, it was like the appetizer before a sumptuous meal. She loved the feel of her calves and Achilles tendons stretching and working as she climbed upward, pumping her arms, throwing one foot ahead, rolling forward smoothly, only to bring the other foot forward, to roll forward yet again....

She was aware of her surroundings; there were still some shallow puddles in the gravel from the thunderstorm that had passed through just after midnight and the westerly wind was brisk, playing along the face of the palisades. But the low-70s sun was warm on her face and neck as she climbed back and forth up the bluff face.

At the same time, though, as she always did when she ran, she was slowly withdrawing into herself, focusing on her body. Not specific parts, like certain aching muscles, or lungs gasping for air, or sweat trickling down her side, or sharp rocks poking her through her shoes; but rather on the whole of her body, on the totality of her experience.

She knew the feeling well. It was what she always sought, was perhaps addicted to, and nearly always achieved when she went for a run, her runner's Zen. It was easy to use words like "trance-like" or "rapturous" or "runner's high" to try to explain the feeling, but they were like trying to describe the Grand Canyon to someone who had never seen it, inadequate at best.

At the top of the bluff she chose to follow the Neshnala Loop Trail clockwise, first taking the half-mile section closely paralleling Rock Creek. On her right was the dense green forest covering the top of the bluff, oaks and maples and ash, with occasional open meadows festooned with wildflowers, while on her left Rock Creek tumbled over rocky shoals, with picnic benches every hundred feet or so.

Ro liked this part of the trail. It was flat, the turns were gentle and there weren't many walkers, so she could really stretch out and gobble up the yards at more than a jog, but not quite a flat out run.

Eventually the trail swung east and dipped and climbed across a series of shallow wooded glens, to finally open into a huge mowed, park-like meadow dominated by Neshnala. The woods surrounding the meadow had lots of old trees, many so big one person couldn't put their arms around them, with tall limbs reaching to fifty or sixty feet high...beautiful and impressive in their own right.

But Neshnala was a giant among them. With a circumference of more than twenty feet, three adult men with linked arms couldn't reach around its great trunk. The gnarled roots at its base were more than forty feet across. Its canopy was nearly two hundred feet wide and reached more than a hundred feet into the sky. And because there were always the thoughtless morons who believed it was cool to carve their initials, or something worse, in Neshnala's side, the tree was surrounded by a six-foot high chain link fence, so no one could in fact touch it.

Ro loved Neshnala.

It had taken her breath away the first time she'd seen it as she stepped off a school bus when her second-grade class took a field trip to visit the tree; for most of the kids it was just another tall tree, they didn't especially see why it was such a big deal. However, Ro did. Of course, its immense presence was awe-inspiring. But what had overwhelmed her then, and what still did, was the tree's great dignity. While she didn't know that word as a six-year old, she knew the feeling it inspired…a sense of admiration, even reverence for not only its great age, but its wisdom. She understood why it had been called "The Tree of Knowledge" by the Native Americans.

As always, she slowed to a walk and circled the tree, taking her time out away from the fence so its presence was less of a distraction. Each time she visited Neshnala she seemed to see something different…. Sometimes it was how the other trees kept their distance, as if out of deference to their wizened neighbor…. Sometimes it was the vibrant green of its canopy, seeming more alive, more energetic than the trees around it…. Sometimes it was the gnarled branches that looked like the knuckles of an old man…. Today she seemed to sense the tree's roots and how profoundly they delved into the life-giving earth below….

And, as always, she stopped on Neshnala's west side, because it was where one of the tree's long branches dipped closest to the ground, perhaps only six or seven feet above her head, so it was where she could feel the most connected to the tree and where a sense of peace and, at the same time, vigor, seemed to spread through her. To her there was no doubt it was coming from the tree, like it was the tree's gift to anyone who was ready to accept it.

After a few minutes Ro closed her eyes and briefly dipped her head to the tree, something she had started years ago. She didn't know exactly why, except it just felt like the right thing to do. Under her breath she muttered, "Respect," then took a step back. Her only regret was she couldn't touch the tree.

Pulling the Gatorade bottle from its holder she took a long drink, then kicked her knees up several times and started her run again, this time turning south to head back toward the bluff. When she reached the edge of the bluff the trail hit a T, with a sign that said the Neshnala Loop continued to the right, to return to the top of the falls, while the Bluff Trail went left.

Ro went left, the trail now just a wide, beaten-down dirt path. By following the Neshnala Loop her run would have been just over two miles, a short one for her. The Bluff Trail continued east along the edge of the bluff, crossed over into the county's adjacent forest preserve, and eventually dropped down the face of the bluff to the Lower Trail, which ran roughly east to west at the base of the palisades. Adding the Bluff and Lower Trails, altogether her run would be closer to five miles, a more respectable distance for her.

She got back to her car at not quite nine-thirty, used the bathroom, finished her bottle of Gatorade, and headed for home and her usual Monday errands. As she left the state park she felt a mild disappointment she hadn't seen the green Dodge.

CHAPTER FIFTEEN
AMBUSHED

Sunday, July 27, 2003, 1 p.m.

The morning had been cloudy and a thunderstorm had passed through a little before noon, threatening to dampen their barbecue, but as Ro arrived at Eddy and Gloria's the sun was out and it was a mild seventy-four degrees. The couple lived in a small, Cotswold cottage-style home in an older neighborhood of Lee's Landing. The front yard was surrounded by a neatly trimmed, waist-high privet hedge, and the front stoop was flanked by two large pots overflowing with colorful petunias and geraniums, both courtesy of Gloria. Tall and slender arbor vitae trees flanked the front corners of the house, adding even more to its English country air.

Ro knew Eddy's patrol car and Gloria's Mazda Protégé would be parked in the garage off the alley behind the house—it was the kind of old neighborhood that still had alleys—so she was a little mystified by the white Toyota RAV 4 parked on the street. Her curiosity was piqued as to who else they might have been invited to their barbecue.

She was wearing what she always wore for casual occasions

like this...loose fitting khaki hiking shorts, a slightly oversized forest green T-shirt, low cut, dark grey walking shoes with no socks, and, of course, her fanny pack.

The front door was open, so she called through the screen door. "Hello!" But, as she expected, no one answered, as both Gloria and Eddy were likely in the backyard.

Letting herself in, she passed down a long hall with the living room off to one side and the dining room off to the other, and into the kitchen at the back to put the cheesecake she'd bought for dessert in the refrigerator. She left the kitchen through the back door, except it was really a side door, so she had to walk down a short walk to reach the actual backyard.

As soon as she rounded the corner Frank Reyner jumped up from where he had been sitting under a big umbrella with Eddy and Gloria, clearly having positioned himself to spot her arrival, and strode toward her. "Hi," he said, with enthusiasm, but also with a touch of uncertainty, as if he didn't quite know what to do or say next, like call her Ro or offer his hand.

Equally nonplussed—she was delighted to see him, but at the same time flummoxed about what to do or say—she managed a wan smile and said, "Hello, Frank," then added, "it's nice to see you."

Oh my god, that's as lame as what I said to him the last time. He's probably thinking I'm some kind of social dolt, she thought. Then, out of a corner of her eye she saw Eddy and Gloria grinning at the two of them, like cat's that had just downed a couple of canaries, which added even more to her discomfort, and suspicion....

Rounding on them with a frown of mock annoyance, she said, "What're you two grinning at?" Then, as if a light had gone on in her head, added, pointing an accusatory finger at Gloria, "Did *you* arrange this?" Gloria was always trying to fix her up.

Gloria feigned a look of innocence and held up her hands in a "not me" gesture.

"In point of fact, it was me," Frank said, with a sort of hang dog look. "So, if you've gotta be mad at somebody, it's me."

She noticed he was wearing khaki hiking shorts, not unlike hers, sandals, and a yellow polo shirt that complimented his outdoorsy tan, which, because the only other time she'd seen him was under the harsh lights of the gas island at TC's, she hadn't noticed. But it was more than his tan she noticed…couldn't help but notice. There were those darn eyes again. While the rest of Frank's face was certainly pleasant, although not what you'd call handsome, it was those eyes, with little laugh lines in the corners that were remarkable. Most guys didn't look at you; their eyes darted here and there, but rarely directly at you. But Frank *was* looking directly at her, his eye contact steady, but, in no way intimidating. Indeed, what those eyes seemed to be saying was, "I am genuinely interested in getting to know you, Ro Delahanty. All I ask is a chance."

Regaining her footing a little, she said, "I'm not mad…. More like confused…."

Eddy stood up. "Let me get you your drink, Ro." Which they knew meant a stubby old-fashioned glass of Chianti…Sonny had introduced her to Chianti. "Then let's sit down and we'll explain."

When they were seated around the glass topped table under the umbrella, each with a fresh drink—Eddy and Gloria together on one side, Eddy with a beer, Gloria with a rum and Coke; Ro and Frank on another, Frank also a beer drinker—Frank said, "I guess I'll start by apologizing to you, Ro. *I* asked Eddy to do this because I wanted to meet you."

Ro gave him one of those cocked-head "Okay, go on, I'm interested" looks.

Apparently encouraged by the fact she didn't appear mad, he smiled and went on. "Eddy and I have been friends for what, sixteen years?" He looked at Eddy, who nodded. "We're both in the Iowa National Guard MP Unit based out of Des Moines.

After I met you last week at TC's, I called Eddy and asked him if he knew you, which, of course he did. Anyway, I also asked him if he could help me get to meet you again." After a brief pause he added, "And so, well, this ambush was really my idea," raising his eyebrows in a gesture that said, but not out loud, "the next move's up to you."

Of course, Ro saw the question in his eyes, but she also saw the hopefulness and, at the same time, fear of being shot down behind those eyes.... *Such expressive eyes*, she thought, remembering how he had impressed her with his genuineness, even during their brief and more or less perfunctory—or at least what she had thought of as perfunctory—earlier meeting.

Maybe because Frank *did* seem so different from other guys, or maybe because she hadn't had a boyfriend of any kind in more than two years; or maybe because she remembered how let down she'd felt when she hadn't bumped into him either time she'd gone to the state park for a run, yes, she'd even gone *again*.... She let her guard down, laughed and said, "Well, Frank Reyner, I'm *glad* you set this up," putting finger quotes around "set this up." Then, without even thinking about it, she added, "Hell, if I'd known Eddy knew you *I* might have asked *him* to set me up with *you*." Which was, of course, the truth....

Everyone laughed, but especially Frank. *Darn those eyes,* Ro thought, *with those wonderful little laugh lines.*

And that set the tone for the rest of the afternoon.

Gloria, who was, as her Swedish name implied, tall, blonde and beautiful, served French bread and artichoke dip, while Eddy hovered over the chicken and beef shish-ka-bobs on the grill.

The conversation was mostly light and casual, with a little gossip about other deputies, some sharing of embarrassing moments each had had, a lot of background stuff on Lee's Landing for Frank's benefit, and a discussion of favorite foods.

Ro did learn some tidbits about Frank. He'd been divorced

108

for eight years; he had a near fifteen-year old daughter who lived with her mother in Des Moines; he'd been with the Iowa DNR for ten years, having just come from Pilot Knob State Park, near Forest City; he and Eddy had been in the National Guard for sixteen years—which Ro mentally calculated made him around thirty-four—he was a sergeant in the guard; and, despite that his name was an Americanized version of a decidedly French *reynard*, which meant fox, his favorite food was Italian. And no, he had not been to Papa Tony's yet....

"You're kidding," declared Gloria. "Papa Tony's is like a local institution. They've been around for as long as I can remember."

"Papa Tony" had five very popular pizza parlor-Italian restaurants in the Illowa area. Papa Tony also happened to be Anthony Mateo Colletta II, Sonny Colletta's grandfather.

And that Frank hadn't yet visited Papa Tony led to his and Ro's first date, initiated by Ro.

"Well," she'd said, "we're just going to have to take care of this serious gap in Frank's Lee's Landing education. I'll treat for pizza next Monday, not tomorrow, a week from tomorrow."

Ro glanced at Gloria, about to add she meant for Gloria and Eddy to come too, but Gloria frowned and quickly shook her head, then grinned triumphantly, as if she'd finally succeeded in "fixing-up" Ro, although perhaps not in quite the way she'd imagined.

Frank wiped his brow with a fingertip and shook off a non-existent drop of sweat. "Whew! And *I* was fretting about how I was gonna ask *you* out."

CHAPTER SIXTEEN
THINKING CHAIR

Monday, Aug. 4, 2003, 4:15 p.m.

Ro and Frank had talked a couple of times on the phone and had arranged to meet at 5:30 at the original Papa Tony's restaurant on Old Post Road. Gloria had been right, Papa Tony had established his first restaurant in Lee's Landing in the late 60s. It wasn't far from Ro's apartment and was relatively convenient for Frank coming in from the state park. Then they'd agreed to go see *The Italian Job*, with Mark Wahlberg and Charlize Theron, discovering a mutual fondness for caper movies.

With Co-Co Woo's interpretation of Haydn's *Cello Concerto* in D playing in the background, Ro was once again standing at the foot of her bed, this time wearing only a pair of cotton briefs, her hands on her hips.

She'd showered, but instead of moussing her hair flat, like she always did before going on duty, this time she'd added some conditioner, fluffed it under the hand dryer into a kind of short shag and even combed some forward in a loose bang. It was decidedly more feminine than her usual look.

Arrayed on the bed were the several possible outfits she'd

chosen and was now agonizing over. Thrown across the pillows was her first choice, the kind of outfit she was most comfortable in, her usual day-to-day "uniform" of loose fitting hiking shorts and a T-shirt. But she knew it was way too casual for "a date." Although she wasn't conscious of it, she had mentally put quotation marks around "a date."

Across the middle of the bed was about as much a polar opposite outfit as Ro could muster...a gray, knee-length skirt, a French blue silky blouse, and a blue blazer, all still in their plastic dry cleaning sheath from the last time she'd worn them several months ago. It was her *de rigueur* for any event involving a church, like a wedding or a funeral.

But she'd pretty much rejected it, as well...way too preppy.

Next was what she thought might be a good compromise for "a date." A pair of new jeans—she hated the newly-faddish ratty jeans look—flats, a white button down blouse, and a dark red—almost matching the color of her hair—open front, cotton sweater, because restaurants and movie theatres were always over air conditioned, and because it would hide the paddle holster and Glock 19 she carried on her left hip. Not too casual, not too yuppy....

Except she knew the outfits themselves weren't the real cause of her agonizing. What was, in fact, the source of her dithering was the pair of bras sitting side by side at the foot of the bed. Neither was a sports bra, her usual choice. On the right was a more or less conventional bra, the kind designed to support her 34 C breasts, yet not call too much attention to them. But on the left was a bra she'd dug out from the bottom of her lingerie drawer. Why she'd saved it she really didn't know; her other bras like this one, along with the thongs and tight T-shirts with deep necklines she'd once worn, had all been pitched a little over two years ago.

It was the kind of bra designed to lift and squish the boobs together, to create a deep and very conspicuous cleavage, to fairly shout "you can have me."

She looked down at her bare breasts. They were not huge, especially compared to many of the girls in her high school class who'd had their bust lines "enhanced," but they were round and full, and yes, sexy…at least she'd been told that more than a few times. Even the memory of a lover gently massaging her breasts, caressing the nipples with his fingers or lips hardened the tips into small peaks.

She closed her eyes and sighed deeply, then, glancing up at the panda, with its inscrutable half-smile, said, "Don't you grin at me like you know something I don't. I'm struggling here." Then she added, "Okay, I guess it's time for The Thinking Chair."

The Thinking Chair was, in fact, a beat-up old — it was what, at least as old as she was? — recliner that now sat in her study across the hall. But, instead of being positioned to look into the room, as a chair typically would, it was turned so its back was to the room and someone sitting in it was looking out the large sliding glass door at the woods behind the apartment, just as it had been similarly positioned in her childhood bedroom to look at the woods behind their house. She'd "inherited" it on her twelfth birthday, when her father had decided to replace it with a new one. Rather than let him throw the old one away, she'd asked for it to be moved to her bedroom; after all, it was the recliner in which as a child she would curl up in his lap and nod off to sleep listening to Mozart or Hayden or Beethoven. Even though Big Mike hadn't sat in it for nearly a decade, she imagined — she was pretty sure it *was* her imagination — whenever she plopped down in the chair she could still catch a faint whiff of the Irish Spring soap he always showered with.

Over the years she'd spent lots of hours in that chair, ironically, though it was a recliner, she'd never reclined it, when she couldn't sleep at night or, like now, when she was wrestling with something.

For some reason she knew she needed to be naked — maybe because she just liked being naked, or maybe because being naked meant she'd stripped away any artifice — and so she peeled off her panties and threw them on the bed between the bras, thinking to herself, *Oh, there's gotta be something symbolic in* that!

Padding across the hall, she dropped into the chair, throwing one leg over an arm, exposing her womanhood. She understood, of course, the two bras were only symbols for what was really troubling her: should she sleep with Frank Reyner? There was no doubt in her mind she *did* want to climb into the sack with him. And, although he'd done nothing to overtly suggest it, she knew at an instinctive level he was attracted to her.

No, she thought, *whether you sleep with Frank isn't the real issue here. You know you want to, and you're pretty sure he wants to. That's not what's bothering you. It's that you haven't been with anyone in over two years, and you know damn well you miss it.... And whether you want to start down* that *road again....*

She looked down at her pubis and the hint of an opening buried between her legs, and imagined someone sliding his hard manhood into that opening. It brought a deep sigh, and even the imagined sensation caused her to get a little wet. *Oh yes, you definitely miss it....*

Several images flashed through her mind in quick succession.

The first, of course, was of Sonny Colletta. She'd lost her virginity to him the summer after she'd graduated from high school. He was her only lover — although she was pretty sure she was not his — through that summer. Sonny was a gentle and attentive lover, and had patiently helped her explore her newly discovered womanhood, which she had embraced with enthusiasm and delight.

Another was…Denny? Danny? Donny? She couldn't remember.... He was a weaselly guy who she'd gone to bed with just once…a one-night stand. He'd been her worst lover ever, basically mounting her, humping her as fast and as hard as he could—although she'd even enjoyed that, at least a little—until he came, then rolling over and going to sleep. Not even a "Wow, that was great!" or a perfunctory "Thank you, ma'am." Fortunately, she'd driven her own car to his apartment, so she'd dressed and left.

And there was Kevin…. He was, like Sonny, more of a lover than a fucker. She'd slept with him not quite a dozen times, each one better than the one before. But he was married—separated, but still married—so that relationship really wasn't going anywhere.

Altogether, over not quite a year, she'd had sex with nearly a dozen different guys, several many times. And what she'd discovered about herself was she *loved* sex. She loved the physicality of it. She loved the passion of it. She loved the intimacy of it. And most of all, she loved the totality of it, how it became all there was in the universe, just a man inside a woman, a woman accepting a man inside of her, each giving lots of pleasure to and taking lots of pleasure from the other. Being honest with herself, she knew she liked sex so much she could easily have become a first-rate slut.

But, finally there was what she had come to think of as The Image…. It was an image of her in a cop's uniform, pulling over a car acting erratically, like it was being driven by a drunk, only to discover the guy behind the wheel was some stranger whose name she couldn't remember but who'd she'd shacked up with the week before. *A first-rate slut….*

But this was old news. She'd been through all this agonizing two years ago, and had made the conscious choice then—a choice she'd never regretted, except maybe until today?—that being a cop who could act like a cop *should* act, without compromise, was way more important to her than getting laid regularly.

And so, for just over two years she'd been celibate, at least

114

insofar as being with a man was concerned.

Returning to the bedroom, she glanced at Peter, understanding now what he'd been grinning about, what he had known but that she had needed to figure out for herself. That was then, this was now. And Frank Reyner was surely anything but a casual lay after a party….

And she understood that, despite her instinctive inclination to want to do so, she couldn't always be in control of what happened in her life.

Grinning back at the panda, she said, "Well, Peter, this might turn out to be a date, or this might turn out to be *a date*…. We'll just have to see, won't we?" The Panda only smiled.

She put away the shorts and T-shirt, hung the skirt, blouse, and blazer back in her closet and started dressing in the jeans and blouse outfit, choosing the bra on the right.

CHAPTER SEVENTEEN
THE DATE

Monday, Aug. 4, 2003, evening

Their timing was impeccable. At 5:27 p.m. Ro turned her red Explorer off Old Post Road and into the spacious Papa Tony's parking lot. Maybe five spaces away she saw Frank's white RAV 4 pulling into another empty spot.

He had just started across the parking lot toward the restaurant's entrance when Ro, stepping out of her Explorer, called, "Hey!"

Turning, his face broke into a big smile. *There are those laugh lines, again!*

"Hey," he said back. He was wearing a short sleeve, striped oxford cloth button down shirt, tucked in, khaki slacks and loafers, but no socks. *A little dressy, but a little casual, too,* Ro thought.

"Wow! You look nice," he said, stepping back and taking her in. As it often seemed to be with Frank, if anyone else had said something like that there might have been some subtle putdown, like she didn't usually look nice. But with Frank there was not a trace of double meaning; it was what it seemed, an honest compliment.

Then he did something strange, extending his left hand, the hand open, as if he wanted to grasp something. It confused Ro at first. It clearly wasn't intended for a handshake...they were a little past a handshake, at least she thought they were. And then she got it. *He wants to hold my hand,* she thought. *Yeah, w-a-y past handshake!* It wasn't a forced gesture, an "I'm trying to push it to the next level" gesture. It seemed entirely natural, like they were just a regular couple meeting for the umpteenth time after work for a drink and dinner.

She found she liked the idea.

They were barely in the restaurant when a huge, deep voice shouted, "Ro!" A tall man with a full head of wavy, snow white hair, a thick white mustache, and equally thick, but still dark eyebrows grasped her in a huge, fatherly hug. Then, turning to Frank and grinning broadly, he threw out his hand and said, "Hi, I'm Papa Tony Colletta."

Taking his hand, Frank said, "Frank... Frank Reyner." There was flash of recognition in Frank's eyes, but it quickly turned to a question, like he was trying to recall something.

"Nice to meet you Frank." Then, glancing from Ro to Frank and back again with a hopeful smile, Papa Tony added, "This a date?"

Ro rolled her eyes, but Frank said, "Yes, sir."

"Good!" Papa Tony said emphatically. Then, putting a hand on Frank's shoulder and moving just a bit closer, he said, slightly sotto voce, "This is a special girl, so you treat her right or you'll have to answer to Papa Tony." But he'd said it with such good humor and genuine affection for Ro that there was no hint of an actual threat.

Going with the moment, Frank said back, "Oh, I will sir."

"Good! Good! Come on," Papa Tony said, turning. "I'll take you to one of my best tables."

The restaurant was huge, maybe a total of sixty tables, but

was artfully divided into sections by half walls topped with ivy covered lattice work so you felt like you were among only half-a-dozen or so tables and not in a big, noisy restaurant. Frank would later be surprised to figure out the ivy was real pots of variegated philodendron, not plastic leaves. The walls were covered with large travel posters with Italian images: Venice's gondolas, Rome's Coliseum, beautiful Lake Como with the towering Alps in the background, a hillside villa surrounded by vineyards in Tuscany.

As they sat down at the table, Ro looked up at Papa Tony. "That was great news about Sonny." Papa Tony was one of the e-mail recipients. Then, turning to Frank, she explained, "Papa Tony's grandson is Sonny Colletta."

With a flash of recognition, Frank said, "The golfer. Didn't I read he won the NCAA championship a month or so ago?"

"You sure did," Tony said, lifting his head with pride.

Ro briefly thought she might let it go at that, but then decided to not explain would be sort of a lie by omission.

"Papa Tony and I and a bunch of others just got an e-mail from Sonny telling us he's going to be ranked the top amateur golfer in the world by the AGA," she said.

"Number one in the world.... Wow! I bet you're proud," Frank said.

"As can be," Papa Tony said, then, handing Ro and Frank menus, added, "The first round's on me tonight. What'll it be?"

"House Chianti," Ro said.

"Make it two," Frank said.

"Coming up," Tony said, moving away.

"Papa Tony's quite a character," Ro chuckled.

"Gloria *did* say Papa Tony's was an institution, but I thought she meant the restaurant."

"She meant both," Ro said. "My family and I have been coming to Papa Tony's for years. He knows everybody by name, and even what their favorite dish is."

"Speaking of 'dish,' what do you recommend?" Frank said, opening the menu.

"Well, I'd say half or more of the folks who come here only order the pizza, which is legendary. And we should try it sometime." She had a brief qualm about using the "we" pronoun and the future tense for what they implied, but then pressed on. "But for your first time here, and especially since you like Italian food, I'd recommend either the spaghetti bolognaise or the baked chicken ziti."

"How about we order one of each and trade back and forth?"

"Okay with me."

Papa Tony returned with their drinks and they fell silent for a moment. Ro watched Frank, who was looking around the restaurant with a curious smile, as if he wanted to see everything. Frank was not like any guy she'd ever met. Even the most seasoned daters had their awkward moments, where a gesture, or something said, or even a look seemed forced, seemed insincere.

And then Ro had a flash of insight that seemed to explain why Frank was so different. *He's like a little boy,* she suddenly thought. *He's just having so much fun with life.*

A teenage girl appeared at the table side. "Hi, Ro," she said with familiarity.

"Hi, Angie," Ro said, then, turning to Frank, added, "Frank, this is Angie, Papa Tony's granddaughter and Sonny's cousin. Angie, this is Frank."

Angie turned to Frank. "Hi, Frank, nice meeting you."

"Nice to meet you, too, Angie."

There was no question she was Papa Tony's granddaughter. She had the same large, expressive eyes and thick, wavy hair, although hers was dark and tumbled down to her shoulders. She was quite beautiful, but in a classic way.

"I hear you're off to college in the fall," Ro said.

"Uh huh, Iowa," she meant the University of Iowa, "for hospitality management, what else?"

"Angie, that's great!" Ro said. "You'll be what, the fourth generation of Colletta restaurateurs?" Then turning to Frank, she explained, "Angie's great-grandfather back in Italy had a restaurant, and her father is co-owner of Papa Tony's."

"Yep, the fourth generation; I guess it's in the blood," Angie said. She took their orders and left.

"Speaking of champions," Frank said, a little unexpectedly. "Congratulations to 'Iowa's Best Shooter.'" He lifted his wine glass in a toast.

"Oh, Eddy told you about *that*," Ro said, trying to sound nonchalant, like it really wasn't any big deal.

"No, he didn't. I'll tell you what he *did* tell me in a sec'. No, I read about the Iowa Shooters championship in the *Des Moines Register*, and remember thinking at the time it was really cool a woman had beaten out all those cops and experienced shooters. Then, when you introduced yourself at TC's, I thought, Delahanty? Delahanty? Why do I know name? It wasn't until after you and the other deputy had driven away it suddenly hit me. 'Oh my god *that* was Iowa's best shooter!'" He paused and frowned. "No, wait, that didn't come out right. I don't mean to say I didn't believe *you* could be the best shooter, it was because I'd in fact *met* the best shooter."

"Is that why you asked Eddy to fix us up?"

"Well, partly.... But that was later, after I'd figured out who you were. You probably wouldn't believe what attracted me to you in the first place."

"You *are* going to tell me."

"It was how you walked across TC's driveway."

Once again Ro had the disconcerting feeling Frank had no clue if anyone else had dropped a line like that it would have had "I'm coming on to you" written all over it. Instead, there was no doubt in her mind he really meant it.

"M-y-y w-a-l-k," she said, stretching it out so it didn't but almost, sounded like a question.

Frank sighed. "Ro, when you came striding across that driveway—and yes, I use the word 'stride' on purpose—everything about you said, 'This woman knows who she is. She has a goal.'"

"So you're saying I walk like a man." It came out sounding a little more defensive than she wanted it to be.

"No! No! Anything but.... I'm gonna use a couple of stereotypes here to make my point, so bear with me. Most females when they walk more or less sashay…they swing their hips, they tend to take shorter steps.... And most guys when they walk, they strut: there's more or less this kind of swagger.... I don't think most girls or most men can help it, they're taught it's how you do it.

"But you, Ro Delahanty, you stride like you're going somewhere, and I don't necessarily mean a place as much as a purpose. So, I was first attracted right off the bat by this strange lady cop coming toward me. Then, later, when I figured out who you were, well...." He held out his hands in an expression that said, "Anyway, that's how I felt...."

"You're weird," Ro said, shaking her head, but also smiling.

"Thank you," he said with a brief nod.

"My *walk*, huh?" Ro said.

Frank raised his brows so his eyes were big and open, and nodded vigorously.... *Just like a little kid might do,* Ro thought.

"By the way," Frank said, "if you don't mind my asking, is Ro a family name?"

"Yes, it is. Most people think Ro is short for Rowena. But my birth name is really Rowan. It means 'little red-headed one,' appropriately enough, and several of my female ancestors on my father's side were named Rowan. Anyway, don't change the subject. So, Eddy *warned* you about me, huh?" she said, taking them back to his earlier promise.

Frank leaned back in his chair and grinned. "Yeah, he did, but not like you're thinking."

Now it was Ro's turn to raise an eyebrow.

"Don't forget, Eddy knows me. He's seen me through my divorce, through the *dating thing*." He said this last with a sardonic tone, like it was something he'd just as soon forget. Ro knew the feeling....

"I'll tell you exactly what he said, although it'll probably scare the bejesus out of you. When I called him and told him I'd met this really cool lady, this *Deputy Delahanty*, and did he know her, and if she wasn't involved could he maybe help me meet her, he started laughing like a hyena! Then I heard him shout, 'Gloria, it's Frank. He's already met Ro and wonders if we can fix 'em up.' And I heard her hoot and yell back, 'Cool! We'll have them over for a barbecue.' Anyway, I got the very distinct impression they'd already been scheming how to get us together.... So that's how we ended-up ganging-up on you."

While Ro had forgiven Eddy and Gloria for their little ruse, she did wonder where this was going, and let it show, "So far you're not scaring me...."

"I know. It's what Eddy said next." Leaning forward, he dropped his voice to a little above a conspiratorial whisper. "Ro, he told me he and Gloria would, of course, help me meet you, but I'd better understand what I was getting into.... That *you* were a very special lady, that you would be perfect for me, and that if I started seeing you it would *not* be something casual."

Now it was Ro's turn to suddenly straighten-up in her chair, only this time in surprise. "Oh," she said, except at the same time quickly understanding her surprise was really that Eddy and Gloria had been right from the start, that somehow she knew she and this man could not ever have just a casual relationship. That idea, though, *did* scare her.

But she also knew she'd done the "casual thing" and had walked away from it because, while it could be a fun and exciting time-filler, it was certainly anything but a soul-filler. And, she suspected, Frank Reyner knew it, too.

Ro looked into Frank's eyes and saw nothing but hope and expectation and caring, maybe even a hint of love — that *was* kind of scary! — but no guile, no hidden agenda. She made a decision....

Briefly agonizing over exactly what to say, she settled on something she hoped was sincere, but not too serious.... Knowing maybe how she said it would be as important as what she said, she allowed her face to relax into a slow smile. "You *didn't* scare me, Frank. In fact, I think I'd very much *like* to see where this relationship goes."

He grinned, a huge devilish grin, the relief in his eyes clear. But then he said something that broke the moment, but which probably needed to be broken at that point. "Oh, Eddy *also* warned me you have a black belt in judo, and you could break every bone in my body if I ever got too frisky with you."

"Oh, *thanks, Eddy!* That's a really great way to start a relationship," Ro said.

They were distracted by Angie delivering their plates of food. The heavy stuff behind them, the conversation while they ate was light and relaxed. They did exchange plates, and Frank pronounced the spaghetti bolognaise "great," but the baked chicken ziti "extraordinary."

Frank was full of questions about Ro's growing up, about her family, about why she wanted to be a cop, about how she got interested in martial arts, in shooting.... In fact, every time Ro tried to steer the conversation away from herself, Frank had a new question to ask about her.

However, Ro was able to wheedle a few tidbits from Frank.... In college he'd started out as a "general major," which really meant he didn't know what he wanted to do with himself, until he took a basic resource management course as an elective that awakened something that led to his becoming a park ranger.

He and Eddy had been in the National Guard for sixteen years, both joining when they were eighteen—so, yes, he was thirty-four, thirteen years her senior, which she was surprised didn't bother her, maybe because there was still so much kid in him—and had been deployed once to Kuwait during Operation Desert Storm, although they hadn't seen any actual combat.

His daughter was named Melissa, but went by Missy; she was fourteen years old and would be a freshman at the prestigious Iowa Academy of Science and Math in Des Moines in the fall.

"She wants to be a geographer," Frank said. "Would you believe it? What fourteen-year-old wants to be a *geographer*?" Yet the pride in his voice was clear. He saw her, usually in Des Moines, every other weekend, and had her for two weeks each summer.

They were just finishing up their lemon gelato dessert when Frank glanced at his watch. "Holy shit, it's nearly eight. We'd better hurry if we're gonna catch the last showing."

As they pushed their chairs back, Frank took three twenty dollar bills from his wallet and dropped them on the little tray Angie had left with their bill...the money included a generous tip. Ro thought about objecting, since she'd been the one to ask him on the date, but let it go.

Moving close to Frank, she said, "Actually, I'm not that much in the mood for a movie tonight."

One eyebrow went up, as if he was silently asking, "Are you saying what I think you're saying?"

"I'd invite myself to your place, but I'd bet it's not quite visitor ready," she said.

Frank rolled his eyes. "Uh, 'not quite' would be an understatement."

"Then let's go to my apartment," she said, this time holding out her hand for him to take.

CHAPTER EIGHTEEN
LOVERS

Monday, Aug. 4, late evening

Ro unlocked the door of her apartment and stepped through, turning and kicking off her flats, flipping them into the corner next to the coat closet. Frank followed suit with his loafers.

She had left a small table lamp on in the corner of the living room. It cast a relaxed, low-key glow over the room.

Turning to Frank, she reached under the left side of her sweater and unclipped the paddle holster with its Glock 19. "Let me get rid of this. I'll be right back," she said, disappearing down a shadowy hallway, which then gave Frank a chance to look around the room....

Where convention would have placed a sofa on the one long wall in the room, Ro had positioned it crossways, making the whole room seem wider. What *was* along the long wall was a twenty-seven inch TV with a combination DVD-VHS player on top, flanked on each side by two tall bookcases filled with CDs, DVDs, and VHS tapes. A low silhouette CD player with attached speakers sat on top of one bookcase.

Moving around the sofa, he meant to satisfy his curiosity

about what kinds of movies and CDs Ro favored, but was instead distracted by three large and colorful poster-size artworks on the wall above the bookcases. All three were cartoon-like…no, not cartoon-like, more video game-like action characters. Glancing at all three, he was impressed by the careful attention to detail and the intensity of the illustrations. One was of a Conan-like warrior, clad in leathers, bulging muscles, a sword hilt visible over his right shoulder, and a wicked spear held at the ready in the other. Another seemed to be a riff on a Flash Gordon-character, clad in a close-fitting, one-piece jump suit with a stylized lightning bolt emblem across the chest. He had a blaster in each hand, and was clearly firing away at some sort of alien invader.

But it was the middle poster that caught his eye. It was Ro, or at least sure looked a lot like her!

The character in the poster definitely had Ro's short red hair, although it looked more like flames haloing her head. While the eyebrows and eyes were much fiercer in the poster, they were still unmistakably Ro's. And she had the same wide shoulder, slightly busty, but narrow-in-the-waist-and-hip physique as Ro.

The Ro-character was clearly charging into some dangerous situation, wearing some kind of quasi-military uniform with a weapon laden tactical vest, a badge-like emblem on the front. Her left hand was firing a huge automatic pistol, a long gout of flame erupting from the barrel. The other was stuck out high and to her right, clenched into a formidable fist, and had apparently just delivered a devastating blow to a bad guy who was out of frame, but whose feet could be seen upended behind her.

Frank cocked his head, hearing what seemed to be several violins quietly playing a soaring melody drifting down the hall, and then what sounded like a door being quietly closed. Although Frank couldn't have named the piece of music — it was the opening chords of Vivaldi's *Concerto for Four Violins* — he found he liked it; it sounded joyful.

Then, hearing Ro pad across the carpeted living room to stand behind him, he said, nodding toward the center poster, "Whoever did that is very talented."

"My best friend Atti Mehra did all three. She'll be a senior this fall at Columbia College in Chicago in computer graphic design. She wants to work in the video game industry."

Still not turning, and again nodding at the middle poster, he said, "That *is* you, right?"

"Yeah," Ro said, with a hint of patient resignation. "She claims someday she's gonna make me into a video game...says she'll call it Bitch Bad Ass.... Just what I need," she added rolling her eyes.

"And I have no doubt you'd be the *baddest* of the bad...."

***

Frank had turned to Ro. They were quiet for just a second, then Frank opened his mouth like he wanted to say something, but Ro just shook her head slightly, as if to say, "Not now." She turned and took the few steps she needed to turn off the one light in the room. Even though the room was now "dark," it wasn't really; there seemed to be just enough dim light from some indeterminate source that they could still see one another and the furniture.

Ro returned to stand in front of Frank, locking her eyes with his. In bare feet they were virtually the same height, so they looked straight at one another. She intended for her eyes to be sending a message like, "I want this. You want this. It's okay."

And what she was sure she saw in Frank's eyes seemed to be a reflection of her feelings. "Let's go there together."

Ro lifted Frank's hands from his sides and placed them on the top button of her blouse. He understood and began to unbutton it slowly. Ro put her hands on her hips and took in a deep breath, swelling her chest, ever so slightly pressing her breasts against his hands.

128

When he was finished unbuttoning the blouse he gently pulled it out of her jeans and Ro shrugged it off. Then, helping him a little, she reached behind her back and undid the bra, but left it still hanging in place on her shoulders.

Frank gently lifted the straps and pulled the bra forward and off Ro's breasts. But, unlike every man who had ever undressed her before, Frank's eyes did not furtively drop to ogle her tits, but continued to stare into her eyes, his expression saying, "I see more to look at in those eyes than anywhere else."

My god, Ro though, *this guy* is *special.*

Reaching down, he unbuttoned and unzipped her jeans, then, gently inserting his thumbs not only under the jeans but the panty tops as well, slowly peeled both down over her hips, dropping them around her ankles. She stepped out of the clothes and kicked them aside.

While he *still* did not look down at her nakedness, he did put his hands lightly on her bare hips and began to pull her forward slowly, turning his head slightly…he wanted to kiss her….

But Ro leaned back ever so slightly and held up one finger between them. "Wait," the gesture said.

She undressed him, first unbuttoning his shirt and pulling it backward over his arms, dropping it in a heap on the floor. Then, like he had done with her, she unfastened his slacks and pulled both the slacks and his briefs down, except there was a little tussle to get the underwear over his now fully erect manhood.

Yet their eyes had still not wandered from one another's.

Stepping out of the heaped pants and underwear, he kicked them back out of the way and stepped closer to Ro. She did the same, then leaned forward and gave him just the slightest kiss on the lips, certainly more than a casual kiss, but not yet a fervent one.

Taking Frank's hand, Ro led him down the hall.

"Are you teasing me?" he whispered, but it wasn't in any

way an accusatory question.

Glancing back over her shoulder, Ro raised her eyebrows and scrunched her mouth into a clownish grin, as if to say, "You bet I am."

The music, now a full orchestra further developing what he recognized as the earlier joyful melody, was coming from the room straight ahead. A door on the right was closed and, although he didn't turn his head, he did note from his periphery the bathroom was on the left.

The bedroom's curtains were open, the glow from a half moon in the clear night sky outside wanly illuminating the room. Although Frank didn't know it, Peter Panda was not at his usual post, but instead now sat comfortably in the recliner across the hall. When Ro had stepped into the bedroom to turn on the stereo, on impulse she picked Peter up, and with a whispered, "Sorry," moved him into the study, where she'd also taken a moment to put her gun away in the gun vault. Maybe she thought Frank didn't need to know she still kept, to say nothing of talked to, her childhood teddy bear. Or maybe she just didn't want the distraction of Peter Panda voyeuristically watching them.

Ro pulled Frank around and smoothly positioned him at the foot of the bed.

Understanding what she wanted when she gave him a gentle shove, he sat down on the bed and, using his elbows and feet, crab-walked backwards until he was lying fully on the bed, his head resting on a pillow, looking up at her. His expression was quizzical, but not confused.

Okay, let's see how good you really are, Ro thought. She stood for a brief moment at the bottom of the bed, her hands on her hips, challenging him to drop his eyes and take in her nakedness. But his eyes never wandered. *You passed*, she thought, but then had a brief twinge of guilt for having given him a quiz he didn't even know he was taking.

Ro climbed onto the bed at his feet. Straddling him, but on her haunches so she was not really touching him, she slowly crawled up his legs. Although keeping eye contact, it was still easy to see his manhood straight and hard and, it seemed to her, quivering ever so slightly.

God, I want you inside of me....

When her womanhood was poised directly over him, she raised her eyebrows slightly and lowered her head just slightly, silently commanding him, "Please enjoy this."

And then she lowered herself onto his stiff cock. Not quickly; not plunging onto him; not just seizing him in an erotic frenzy... *Fuck me!* But slowly, oh so slowly, millimeter by millimeter, his hardness gradually, oh so gradually, slipping into her.

It had been so long...so long since she'd felt a man inside of her womanhood, his hunger wanting her, her hunger wanting him, his hardness penetrating her; not just her cunt, but like it was filling her whole body with pleasure....

She was very wet—she had always gotten wet easily—so that Frank slid into her so effortlessly....

Using all the muscle power running had developed in her upper thighs, she leisurely descended on him, teasing him, and, at the same time prolonging his—and her—enjoyment.

Frank didn't move.... He didn't suddenly start bucking under her, trying to stick himself into her faster than she wanted him to, for which she was grateful. *He gets it*, she thought with amazement. *He's content to let me pleasure him*; except, of course, she was thoroughly enjoying herself as well.

While Frank didn't move, he did stare up at her, his eyes now wide with delight, his mouth open in wonderment, his breath coming in short gasps. He was trying so hard to hold back....

Finally, she could lower herself onto him no further; she could not take any more of his rigidity inside of her, her thighs resting across his pelvis.

131

Then she tightened herself around his cock, a special skill she had been told only a few women could accomplish. For just a second or two she enjoyed his rigidity, sticking deeply into her womanhood, filling her...filling her....

But then his cock convulsed. She could feel it begin to swell at the base, then quickly throb and finally explode inside of her.

That's when Frank couldn't help himself.... Where his hands had been gently holding the outside of her thighs, as if he could in some way enhance the delightedly measured way of her taking him in, he suddenly gripped her hips hard and pulled down, and, at the same time, arched his back, thrusting his hips upward, trying vainly to penetrate her even more deeply.

But he didn't utter a sound. He just frowned in total concentration and worked his mouth in a silent shout of utter ecstasy, as his cock pulsed inside of her, once, twice, three times, four times....

She felt it and it was wonderful! His cock swelling inside of her and his man essence squirting into her was like someone had stuck a super-soaker into her cunt and was pulling the trigger, again and again...

For many seconds Frank just stared up at her, a mixture of complete astonishment and at the same time total gratification in his eyes. Reaching out, he pulled Ro down on top of him. Of course, it also ever so slightly pulled her hips up and away from him and he felt, and she felt, his now flaccid cock slip out of her.

With one hand he guided her head to rest against his neck and shoulder, with the other he pushed on the small of her back so her breasts were crushed against his chest. Her crotch, still wet and sticky with her aroused womanhood and his expended manhood, rested on his hip, her long and powerful legs now stretched out against his. He wanted to experience every inch of Ro's breathtaking body.

Then bringing both hands up, he lifted her face so he could

look into your eyes. "You're *unbelievable*," he whispered hoarsely, his eyes filled with respect and, there was no mistaking it now, a hint of love. At least for the moment the idea didn't scare her....

And then he kissed her; not a gentle, tentative kiss, nor a demanding, hungry "I want to possess you, and I want you to possess me" kiss; while it was most certainly a deeply passionate kiss, at the same time it was a respectful, admiring kiss.

After a few moments they broke the kiss and Ro tumbled onto her side next to him.

Turning to look at her, Frank said, "I'm sorry."

Screwing up her face in a frown of incredulity, Ro said, "Sorry for *what?*"

"For not staying with you, not pleasing you more...."

Pushing herself up, Ro settled into a lotus position, her hands on her hips, now fairly demanding Frank look at her, which he finally did.... His eyes fell and rested on her breasts, full and round, with their tiny red mountain tops, lingering there for a long time, then drifted lower to gaze at her exposed womanhood, droplets from their spent passion glistening on her pubis, the pinkness of her womanhood inviting. Ro didn't feel like this man was lustfully ogling her sensuality—she'd seen *that* kind of look before—but rather was admiring her with the kind of respect and awe he might have while looking at *The Pieta*.

Leaning forward to sort of get in his face, Ro said with a playful grin, "Well, Frank Reyner, in case you haven't figured it out, it was *my* intent to please you, which I *do* think I did pretty darn well. And have no doubt, mister; *you* are going to pleasure *me*...a lot! Later."

CHAPTER NINETEEN
APPOINTMENTS FOR US TIME

Tuesday, August 5, 2003, morning

And he had: twice, each time "staying with" Ro for sustained periods that had surprised even him, bringing her to agonizing and ecstatic climaxes again and again.

What is that smell? Coffee? But there's some kind of clean, soapy smell, too?

Frank opened his eyes and saw Ro standing in the doorway of the bedroom wearing dark green cut-off sweat shorts and a red T-shirt, her hair still wet from a shower. The clean smell was coming from her. *I know that smell,* he thought. *It's Ivory soap. We used to bathe Missy with it when she was little.*

It made him smile. Not because he thought of Ro as a little girl — this woman was definitely *not* a little girl — but because of the irony that for him the scent would now be associated with two amazing memories.

The coffee smell was coming from the two mugs Ro was holding, which also made him smile.

Even though it was loose fitting, her T-shirt did not hide she was braless, her breasts swaying ever so provocatively when she moved.

She was looking down at him, her "cop face" gone, now relaxed into a merry Irish grin.

"I thought you might like some coffee," she said, holding out a heavy, white mug. "It's black, but I can get milk and sugar if you want."

"Black's fine, thanks," he said, sitting up and reaching for the cup. He was still naked, though modestly covered by Ro's dark blue, soft jersey sheets, except those breasts were causing some at this point unwelcome stirrings. "You're the best thing I've woken-up to in a very long time," he said, looking up at Ro earnestly.

"Oh, that's too bad," she said with a brief frown, then grinned. "But thanks for the compliment."

"What's 'too bad'?"

"That there hasn't been someone special for you in a while."

Frank pushed himself back to lean against Ro's pillows.

Now in the daylight Ro saw for the first time how lean Frank's body was; narrow in the shoulders and chest, flat bellied, sinewy—oh, she remembered those arms around her just fine—but not muscular. *I'll bet he doesn't weigh much more than I do,* she thought.

He patted the empty section of the bed next to him, then realizing the gesture might be taken more than one way, quickly added, "Just sit and talk."

Feigning disappointment, like she had hoped he'd meant the other way, Ro sat on the edge of the bed and gazed at Frank, her brows raised slightly, as if to say, "Okay, what do you want to talk about?"

Frank took a sip of the coffee, then said, "But there *was* someone special in bed with me last night."

She blushed slightly and just nodded, not quite knowing what to say.

"Ro, making love with you—and I *do* mean 'making love,' because for me it was way more than just sex—was fantastic. And I certainly expect we'll do it again...I hope quite often," he said, wiggling his eyebrows in an exaggerated lecherous smirk.

It made Ro giggle. *You're damn right 'quite often,'* she thought.

"But in a way that's the easy part. The hard part is we just sort of got dropped into each other's lives, in both cases I'm sure quite unexpectedly, and now we gotta somehow deal with the ripples...." He trailed off, frowning slightly. "Does that even make sense?"

Swinging around, Ro took a cross-legged position on the bed, her look now serious. "It makes perfect sense. And, by the way, that *was* pretty poetic for a tree hugger."

Which made Frank grin in turn.

"Frank, we've all got a past of some kind, but it doesn't have to get in the way," Ro said.

"I agree with that. But, we're also kind of the result of that past." Pausing, Frank sighed. "Look, all I'm trying to say here is I *do* want to know more about the now Ro, and I hope she will not be afraid to tell me things about the yesterday Ro that will help me appreciate the today Ro all the more."

Damn you, Frank Reyner, Ro thought. *Quit trying to make me fall for you, 'cause it just might be working.*

Pausing again, Frank threw his hands out in a gesture of openness and said, "So, sauce for the goose.... No, Ro, there hasn't been anyone special for the last two years. After the divorce.... By the way, do you know why I got a divorce? Because my wife fell in love with someone else...another woman.... That was eight years ago, and they're still together." There was no trace of bitterness or recrimination in his voice Ro could sense. In fact, quite the opposite, it seemed to her more like he was glad for his ex that she had found someone special.

"Anyway, after the divorce I dated for a while, and there

were a couple of girlfriends I saw sort of regularly. Then I did live with somebody — she lived with me in fact — for a year-and-a-half, but she didn't want to move to Pilot Knob with me. That was just over two years ago and I haven't dated anyone, let alone been with anybody, since."

Ro shook her head and then pointed at Frank. "Two years? You're not fibbin' to me, are you?'

"I took the job as the ranger at Pilot Knob in March of '01. She came to visit a couple of times in April, but then told me there was no way she could leave her job and her friends in Des Moines to live out in the woods." He paused a second, shaking his head, then went on. "Except, I don't think it's the real reason she dumped me."

"Oh?"

Frank shrugged. "I think it was because I wasn't ambitious enough for her. She was always after me about going for my masters and applying for supervisory jobs with the DNR. When she figured out I really *liked* being just…" — he put air quotes around "just" — "a park ranger…well, it was bye-bye."

"Spring two years ago…I'll be damned," Ro said, shaking her head. She then paused for a long while, buying time by sipping her coffee, but still looking at Frank, her brows shifting in and out of a frown of consternation. Finally, making her own decision to share, she said, "Sonny Colletta was my first serious boyfriend. We were together during the summer of 2000, right after we both graduated from high school. In the fall he went off to Arizona State and really got into the whole college golf lifestyle big time — I don't blame him for that, it *was* his world — but we just kind of stopped seeing one another.

"Anyway, that fall I started at Mississippi Valley Community College over in Illinois in their criminal justice program, but like a lot of freshmen I discovered partying. Let's just say I partied pretty enthusiastically that whole school year, but then figured out it wasn't really the direction I wanted my life to go and so made a change."

Leaning forward, she put her hand on his cheek, pulled him close for a small but sincere kiss, then whispered, "The fact is, Frank Reyner, *you're* the only one *I've* woken-up beside in two years as well." Then, wrinkling her nose, she looked him up and down and said, "Eew, you need a shower; you still smell like sex!"

Jumping off the bed, Ro rummaged in a drawer of her dresser and threw some clothes at Frank. "These cut-offs and T-shirt should fit. You take a shower and I'll make us some breakfast. Omelet okay?"

Throwing back the sheet and scooting across the bed, he said, "Omelet's fine. Hmm, champion at judo and shooting, *and she cooks....*"

As she started down the hall toward the kitchen, Ro called over her shoulder, "I think you'll find *she's* a whole lot better at the judo and the shootin' than at the cookin' stuff...."

***

Twenty minutes later, clad in grey cut-off sweats and a white T-shirt—he'd noted every t-shirt of Ro's he'd ever seen was a plain, solid color, no sports drink or rock band logos, no races she'd been in—Frank padded into the kitchen to find her pouring several whipped eggs into a wide, shallow omelet pan on the stove. Nearby on the counter were small bowls of crispy diced bacon, chopped onions, chopped tomatoes, chopped mushrooms, chopped green peppers, and grated yellow cheese. A fresh pot of coffee was just sighing into the finale of its brewing cycle.

Gesturing to a toaster, Ro said, "You can start the toast." Then, pointing to the bowls, she added, "What do you want in your omelet?"

"Heavy on the bacon and cheese, and a few onions," he said.

Ten minutes later they were sitting at the dining room table,

Frank with his bacon and cheese omelet, Ro with her vegetarian omelet, a plate of toast between them and fresh mugs of coffee within reach. After several forks full of omelet, Frank said, "There is one more thing you need to know, Ro. I'm in Des Moines three weekends a month. Two of them I spend with my daughter, the other is my guard weekend."

"Well, then, we're just gonna have to make appointments for our 'us time,' aren't we?"

***

Which was what they did. They figured out Frank usually got back from Des Moines a little before dinner time on Sunday night, and since that was Ro's night off, he would come directly to her apartment, where she would have something for him to eat and then Sunday night would be their night.

As it turned out over the following weeks and months, from time-to-time they also found a mid-week night they could be together, and every now and then even arranged a stolen "afternoon delight."

CHAPTER TWENTY
PETER PANDA

Tuesday, August 5, 2003, late morning

After Frank left for the ranger station to change into his uniform and go to work, Ro cleaned-up the kitchen and changed the bed, then went into the study and fired up the computer. She read and answered an e-mail from Sonny. He was staying on in Japan for a few weeks to appear in some exhibition matches sponsored by a Japanese company called Migumi, which he even carefully explained was pronounced "my-GOO-me," not "my-GUM-me." Ro recognized the name as associated with musical instruments — didn't they make keyboards? — so wondered why they were sponsoring golf matches.

She was a little surprised to see an e-mail from Atti, as she hadn't had one in nearly a week. Atti was just back in Chicago from India, but a little cryptically said she was going to be out of town again rather than making a trip to Lee's Landing before school started in a few weeks. Ro was just a little miffed by that; they'd been friends for ten years and Atti was one of the few people Ro thought she could tell anything to. She wanted to share the news about Frank, but didn't want to do it in an e-mail.

140

She's probably hooked-up with another lead guitarist, Ro thought. *She's always had a thing for guitarists.*

Ro also checked her online class's discussion forum.

Her responses to Sonny, Atti, and her class posts were hardly more than courteous acknowledgments…because she knew all along she was just trying to keep busy to avoid having to go get Peter Panda out of the recliner where she'd placed him last night and explain herself to him.

With a sigh of resignation she put the computer in sleep mode, pushed the office chair back from her desk, padded across the study, and slid down to a cross-legged position on the floor in front of the recliner, her back to the sliding glass door.

Peter, who was resting in the left corner of the chair, stared through the glass at the trees behind her. Ro had no doubt he was pouting and studiously ignoring her.

"I'm sorry, Peter," she said. "I should have introduced you to Frank and introduced Frank to you." She waited a second, hoping Peter would say something. He didn't.

"I know you're mad at me. You've got a right to be."

She paused for a moment. "No, I'm *not* embarrassed by you. Is *that* what you think?"

Pause. "What do you mean, 'If I'm not embarrassed, then what am I afraid of?' I'm not scared." Which she knew was bullshit the second the words left her mouth.

Pause. "I'm not scared of Frank. He's a really nice guy, for a change."

Then, after a long moment in which Ro had no doubt Peter had given her an accusatory "don't kid me" stare, she closed her eyes and let out a surrendering sigh. "Oh hell, Peter, I am *scared to death* of Frank Reyner! What if he's not really as nice as he seems and he's just using me? God, I'd hate him for that! And I'd hate myself for letting him. Or maybe *I'm* just using him. Did you ever think of *that*? It wouldn't make me very nice, would it? But…."

141

It was hard for her to say. "But…what if he really *is* as nice as he seems and I fall for him? *That* would really screw things up."

Pause. "How? By…by…. Look, I'm finally getting my life together, and he'd be a…. He'd be a…*a distraction!*"

Long pause, as Ro blinked at the teddy bear, like she was trying to work out something he'd said. "I hate it when you're right all the time, you know that? Of course, I can't just tell him to 'take a hike'." She put air quotes around "take a hike." "It's too late, and you damn well know it."

Pushing herself up, Ro picked-up the teddy bear and started across the room. "Okay, let's get you back where you belong. I promise the next time Frank comes over you two will be introduced." Pause, then she touched her little finger to Peter's furry paw. "Yes, pinky swear."

As she was settling Peter in his accustomed spot on the dresser in the bedroom, she looked down at the teddy bear with a frown of surprise. "Ohhh? When Frank's here you *want* to go sit in Dad's chair because it would embarrass you to watch us. How would *you* know what we're doing?"

The teddy bear just smiled his enigmatic smile, as if to say, "You might be surprised at what I know."

***

Frank was prompt: His knock on her apartment door was at precisely 3:30, which was when Ro'd asked him if he could stop by for coffee when she'd called just before lunch. "There's someone I need to introduce you to," she'd said, perhaps a little cryptically.

"Hi," Frank said when she opened the door. It was a light "Hi," an *I'm curious* "Hi," but not an *I'm worried* "Hi." He was still wearing his park ranger's uniform, including the sidearm.

Ro, on the other hand, couldn't quite hide her concern. "Thanks for coming by on such short notice," she said.

Frank snorted, "Hunh, as if I need an excuse to come see

142

you." Then, sniffing the air with a smile, he added, "Hmmm, somebody's been baking."

"Some cinnamon rolls to go with our coffee," Ro said. "Not homemade like my dad would do, though; mine are from one of those tubes you get in the dairy case."

"Well, they *still* smell good."

Halfway through the door he stopped, listening, then frowned and turned toward the CD player on the bookcase as a string quartet started into what sounded like an energetic work of some kind. "I never been much of a classical music guy, but I'm pretty sure I've heard that before. What is it?"

"It's the opening movement of Haydn's *Emperor String Quartet*," Ro said. "You've probably heard it in a movie sometime. It's kind of a cliché for whenever they want to portray a scene at a high class party they usually have a string quartet playing Haydn."

"Well, it's beautiful."

"I'm glad you like it."

Taking Frank by the hand, Ro led him across the living room and down the short hall toward the bedroom, but stopped at the doorway, then gently pushed him through first.

What had been more or less indistinct shadows the night before — at the time he had, of course, been more focused on his companion than the details of the room — were now clear. The queen size bed was to the left of the door, facing a double-size window looking out on a green wall of trees. Hanging on the wall on the other side of the bed were the two large, framed Ansel Adams prints; they somehow cast a relaxing aura over the room. The closet, with a full length mirror attached to the door, was immediately on his right. Below the window was a wide, low six-drawer dresser. But the most striking feature of the room — which Frank was absolutely sure had not been there last night — was a three-foot tall, black and white Panda bear on top of the dresser, resting in a corner from where he could survey the entire room.

Ro sighed audibly, as if she were mustering some courage. "Frank, this is Peter Panda. Peter's been my friend since I was two years old. He's…. He's…." She paused, like she was trying to figure out how to succinctly explain the teddy bear. Then, as though she'd suddenly had an insight, added, "He's my Wilson… you know, like from the Tom Hanks film *Cast Away*."

Without missing a beat Frank let go of Ro's hand and, striding around the bed, bent down so he was eye-to-eye with Peter. "Nice to meet you, Peter," he said. Then, reaching out with his right hand, touched the teddy bear's right paw, like they were shaking hands. "I'm Frank." After a brief silence he said, "Oh, really. Well, thank you, that's very nice to know." Then, following another short pause, he added, "Okay, see you later."

Turning to Ro, with a grin Frank said, "Let's go; you know we disturbed his nap." As they walked down the hall toward the kitchen, Frank said with an exaggerated sigh, "Whew. I just spent the last two hours driving around the park looking for someplace to hide the body."

Ro gave him a suspicious frown.

"Of the 'other boyfriend'" — he put air quotes around "other boyfriend" — "I was afraid I was going to have to shoot after you introduced me to him."

"Very funny!"

There was a plate of the icing drenched, still warm cinnamon rolls and two empty mugs for coffee waiting on the dining room table.

Ro poured the coffee then sat down opposite Frank, studying his expression. She could find no hint of anything like "What did I get myself into with this crazy lady who talks to a three-foot teddy bear?"

Frank, reading her concern, his expression soft and understanding, said, "Ro, when I was a kid I had this big old

144

black lab. Her official name was Tammy; I have no idea how we came up with that. But we called her Sloppy because she loved to give everyone, especially me, big sloppy kisses. She was my best friend. I told her everything and she would sit patiently and look at me as if she understood every word I was saying. I couldn't tell you how many secrets I shared with her. She had this uncanny instinct for knowing when I most needed one of those sloppy kisses or for her to just lay her head in my lap to let me know everything was okay."

Damn you, Frank, you're not supposed to know me that well! But I'm glad you do.

"Peter was taking his nap. That's what he told you?" Ro's voice clearly suggesting she hoped it was all Peter had said.

"Uh, no-o-o," Frank said. "He told me he'd noticed you were smiling a lot more since you'd met me."

Ro jumped up, and with exaggerated steps stalked around the wall separating the kitchen from the living room. Turning, she called down the hall toward the bedroom, "Boy, Peter, I can't trust you with *any* of my secrets!" But there was more merriment in her voice than anger.

CHAPTER TWENTY-ONE
FIRE IN THE BELLY

Wednesday, August 20, 2003, 9:45 p.m.

The two dozen Boy Scouts and their leaders had left over an hour ago, among them firing off more than a hundred light-load nine millimeter rounds down range. Most had at least hit their paper targets; a few had been close to, or even in, the target's bulls eye. Of course, they had all been thrilled by the experience of shooting a "real" gun, and, Ro and Pops Waters fervently hoped, had also been equally impressed by the life-or-death importance of safely handling a dangerous handgun they had stressed in the firearms safety class.

The Fort Armstrong County Sheriff's Department held quarterly gun safety clinics, but would also schedule one for a group of at least ten, depending on range availability. The group tonight, a combination of three scout troops from Gilbert, was one of the latter.

Although she was in uniform—she was on duty in a little over an hour—but would have worn the uniform anyway, for this particular event Ro was a volunteer helping Pops Waters, who was the official range safety officer, with both the classroom portion of the session and with managing the shooters. Ro had taken and passed the National Rifle Association's online range safety officer course and now just needed to have Pops certify she had ten hours of "assistant" range officer experience to also become a certified range safety officer in her own right. As such, she could then conduct the safety classes for the department on her own and get paid for them, although that was not why she wanted to do it.

Ro and Pops were on the lower level of the new shooting range located off Fairgrounds Road, just north of Lee's Landing. They'd set-up a pair of long folding tables facing one another in the foyer behind the firing line and just outside of the closed and locked gun vault, to clean and put away the Berettas they'd used for the shooting practice. The official deputy's issue weapon prior to the Sig .357's, the department had decided rather than sell off the "retired" Berettas they'd keep them for backup and for occasions like gun safety classes and clinics.

One of the strict requirements at the range was that before any shooter could leave the firing line they had to eject the magazine, even if they "knew" it was empty, and rack the slide to make sure there was not a live round in the pipe. Only then could they lay the magazine and gun down on the shelf and walk away.

After everyone was gone Ro and Pops had collected the guns and magazines, most of which still had one or more live rounds, and arrayed them on their work tables. Both Ro and Pops had rolled their sleeves up to their elbows and were wearing aprons to protect their uniforms from the gun oil.

Of course, she had taken apart, cleaned, and reassembled her own weapons hundreds of times since she'd first learned to shoot with her dad's .410 shotgun when she was ten. Unlike many shooters, Ro enjoyed the cleaning part of the shooting experience nearly as much as the actual shooting. Somehow, she felt that handling the weapon's working parts helped her more fully understand it and appreciate it as a tool.

Each time they picked up a gun they first double-checked that the magazine was out and there was no cartridge in the tube. When they were done cleaning and reassembling each gun they reloaded its magazine and then laid the two side by side on a wheeled cart between them that would later be rolled into the gun vault for storage.

Earlier they'd chatted about how the class went — well, they thought — and if Ro could help with the next regularly scheduled class — yes, she could — but then had been quiet for a while.

Finally, Pops said, not looking up from what he was doing, trying to make it sound more like a casual observation than the question it really was. "I understand you haven't put in for time off to go to Houston yet."

Pops — Sergeant Cyril Waters — was a forty-year veteran of the sheriff's department, having become a deputy in 1963 when he'd returned home from serving as a marine in Vietnam. He even pre-dated the Sheriff Lefty Struve era, let alone the current sheriff, Mark Ballard. A little taller than Ro, he still wore his completely white hair in a short military style, parted on the right, and sported a full white mustache…a neatly trimmed mustache was the only facial hair the department allowed on deputies. He was the department's official armorer, which was his capacity tonight, as well as the new deputy's training officer. Pops didn't do patrol duty anymore.

Of course, she knew he was talking about the U.S. Sports Shooter's League national competition in October, which she had automatically qualified for as a state champion.

Ro smiled to herself and, without looking up from her own work, simply said, "Not going."

That did bring Pops' head up, his deep gray eyes wide in surprise. "Really…." Then, after a slight pause and with a frown of disbelief, added, "Why *wouldn't* you go?"

Ro put down the cleaned pistol she had just finished assembling and turned to Pops. She liked Pops and wanted him to understand, so her expression was open and friendly.

"Several reasons, Pops," she said. "First, I didn't want to ask for time off. I've only been on the job a couple of months, so it seemed to me too much like asking for special favors."

"But you've been with the county more than two years; what about vacation time?'

"I used it last spring to go to Des Moines a week early and practice on their course."

"Makes sense…. But this is something really special. You'd be representing the department, so I'm sure Mark would give you a leave of absence, no problem."

Ro was equally sure Pops was right; she probably could get the time off if she tried. But she also knew it wasn't her real dilemma.

"In reality, Pops, I don't *want* to go," Ro finally said, giving him a steady gaze.

"Ohhh…."

"Pops, during the practice week I must have shot off five or six hundred rounds. Between the ammo and the hotel and meals, it took a big chunk out of my savings. To really compete at that level you've gotta be a pro with lots of sponsors. Johnna Mack was the host pro and couldn't compete. She's been shooting *full-time* for fifteen years. If she had been able to compete she'd have beat the pants off me."

"Ahh, I'm not so sure of that."

"I am. I bet she fires five hundred or more rounds *a week* in practice; I'm lucky if I can get in half that much *in a month*. Anyway, *this* is what I want to do," she added, gesturing to her uniform with a wave of her hand. "*Not* to be travelling all the time and having to kiss-up to a lot of sponsors."

In a back corner of her mind she was thinking of Sonny

149

Colletta, who *did* love that other side of competition…not her, though.

With a nod, Pops said, "Well, *that* I can understand. While I'm sure glad you want to be with the department, you know I *do* think if you put your mind to it you *could* be a world class shooter."

"Maybe," she agreed, sort of, but then added, "But the truth is, Pops, I don't have the fire in the belly to compete at that level. All I wanted when I entered the state competition last spring was to prove to *myself* I was the best shooter I could be *for this job.*" Then, with a slow shake of her head, she added, "I don't *need* to show the whole world how good I am."

Pops smiled broadly and nodding with incredulity said, "You're something else, Deputy. Most people's egos would never have let them walk away from a chance to be the best in the world at something."

Ro just shrugged.

Checking his watch, Pops said, "Hey, look at the time. You're on duty in less than an hour. You'd better go clean-up."

Glancing around at what looked like a mess of assembled guns, partially assembled guns, gun parts, rags and cleaning equipment, Ro started to stand, but said, "I can help you clean up."

"Nah, I can finish up here in maybe three-quarters of an hour. You get going."

"If you're sure," Ro said, pushing back her chair and tossing her apron on the table. She retrieved and strapped on her gun belt, then turned toward the bathrooms at the other end of the foyer. It took a couple of vigorous scrubbings to get the oil and the oil smell completely off her hands.

Emerging from the bathroom, she turned to go up the nearby stairs to the upper foyer and her patrol car in the parking lot in front of the building, but then called back. "Good night, Pops."

150

"Good night, deputy," he called back with a wave.

CHAPTER TWENTY-TWO
10-14 — PROWLER

Wednesday, August 20, 2003, 10:58 p.m.

Ro turned the patrol car right, westbound onto Fairgrounds Road from the shooting range's parking lot, heading for her patrol area in the western part of the county. She was just reaching for the car's microphone to make her 10-41call—*beginning tour of duty.* She'd already logged in as *In service* on the MDT when something caught her attention on the periphery of her vision to the right.

The not quite year-old regional shooting range was only the first phase of a new law enforcement campus being built on county-owned land next to the county fairgrounds on the outskirts of Lee's Landing. Construction had started on the second phase, a new regional jail, and they were waiting for final approval of the plans for the third phase, a new sheriff's department headquarters.

The area just west of the shooting range was a large construction zone, surrounded by one of those temporary chain link fences held down by sandbags. A full moon easily illuminated parked heavy equipment and piles of building materials, but also cast deep shadows between.

What had caught Ro's notice was the gate into the construction zone appeared to be partway open, and there had been what seemed to be a flash of red light near the back of the shooting range building, almost like someone had briefly tapped on a vehicle's brake lights.

Slowing the patrol car, she twisted to her right to look more closely, scanning for any movement or another flash. There was none.

"Probably nothing," she muttered to herself.

While not all change necessarily means trouble, for a cop, things that seem out of place means stop and take a look, check it out....

Pulling over on the right shoulder, Ro turned the patrol car around. When she got to the driveway leading into the construction site, now on her left, she turned off the headlights.

If some unauthorized person's on the site, no sense warning 'em I'm coming, she thought.

Stopping in front of the gate, she picked up her microphone. "Armstrong One-Nine."

"One-Nine go," the dispatcher acknowledged. It was Lisa Jarvis; Gwen Teague apparently wasn't at the dispatcher's desk quite yet.

"Checking a possible 10-14" —*prowler*—"behind the new shooting range off Fairgrounds Road. 10-78" —*send backup*— "10-40" —*silent, no siren.*

"One nine, 10-78 10-40," Jarvis confirmed.

Sliding out of the patrol car, she pushed the gate open slowly, making sure it didn't squeal. Getting back in the car she put it in gear and let it roll forward slowly at idle speed.

Front, right, left, rearview side mirrors; front, right, left, rearview side mirrors...

The completed shooting range was on the east side of the site, now to her right, and the under construction jail was on the western side, now on her left. The site for the future sheriff's headquarters was in between, which was where most of the building materials had been stacked and equipment parked, partially obscuring her view of the shooting range. The driveway she was negotiating was on the new jail side of the storage area.

What was that? She thought she'd seen a tiny red glow through a space between a parked front-end loader and a stack of concrete blocks, ahead and off to her right, behind the shooting range.

There it was again.... *Jesus,* she thought, *whoever's out there's smoking a cigarette!*

In order to get to where she figured the intruder was lurking, she'd have to drive the patrol car another hundred plus feet, then turn right for yet another hundred feet or more behind the construction equipment. Knowing the car's crunching on the gravel drive, to say nothing of the rumble of its engine and its bright white panels and distinctive silhouette lit-up by a full moon would alert the intruder to her presence, she stopped the car, turned it off, and decided to approach whatever was out there on foot.

Ro left her mini-light in its pouch on her belt, as the moonlight threw more than enough light to see where she was going. She did not draw her weapon.

Figuring that hunching over and furtively dashing from cover to cover, military style, might only draw attention, Ro walked upright and slowly, keeping to the shadows as much as possible, moving as silently as she could through the grass and weeds, avoiding the gravel driveway itself.

Turning to her right behind the construction equipment, she could see what appeared to be a pair of light-colored cargo vans parked side-by-side maybe forty yards ahead behind the building, their rear double doors open wide. *That'd certainly account for the brake light glow....*

Suddenly a shadowy figure emerged from in front of one of

the vans…. There was a brief red glow from the cigarette, clearly illuminating a face hidden by some kind of mask. She could also see the distinct silhouette of a short, carbine-like rifle slung over his shoulder.

Shit!

Sliding into a shadowy area near a ten-foot high stack of piping, Ro pressed the transmit button on the microphone clipped to her right shoulder epaulet and whispered, "One-Nine. 10-32" — *man with a gun*— "I say again, 10-32."

"10-04 One-Nine," the dispatcher, now Gwen Teague, said into Ro's earbud, her voice tense.

What the hell's going on here? Two vans…. This guy's not alone. Where're the others? What the hell are they after?

And then she knew. *Ah, the guns!*

Someday, when the new sheriff's headquarters was done, the shooting range's gun vault would stow all of the department's weapons, including the deputy's issue Sigs, shotguns and SWAT-style carbines. For now it usually held only the fifty retired Berettas and a dozen replica Western-style Colt 44s, leftovers from former Sheriff Lefty Struve's "posse," a showy, horse mounted group of deputies in full Western get-up, complete with tie-down gunfighter-style holsters and Colts, that made appearances in parades and county fairs. Hardly a worthwhile objective for a grab….

However, ever since the infamous shootout with some bank robbers in North Hollywood six years ago, where the bad guys equipped with assault rifles had completely outgunned local cops and their small bore handguns, there had been lots of interest in equipping officers with more potent firepower.

The Iowa State Police had set-up a series of demonstrations around the state for local law enforcement agencies to test a variety of such weapons…several types of assault rifles, some even with full auto capability, and sniper-type long guns. The eastern Iowa region's demonstration was scheduled for this coming Saturday at the Regional Firearms Facility.

The guns for this weekend must've arrived today, Ro figured. *That would be a valuable target.*

Deciding speed was now more critical than stealth, Ro stepped into the driveway and started walking quickly toward the vans, drawing her weapon, but still holding it down at her side. A part of her grasped she was supposed to be frightened; after all she'd been on the job barely eight weeks and was facing her first armed bad guy. Some cops went years before ever drawing their weapon.

She was keyed up and alert…adrenaline was certainly taking care of that…. But she was not frightened…or, if she was she was not conscious of it…. There was this armed perp who wasn't supposed to be there, and there were probably others…. *They* were her center of attention right now, not her own feelings….

When she was a few feet behind but slightly to the right of one of the vans — she was surprised the intruder still hadn't heard her; everything about his demeanor said this guy was bored and inattentive — she moved to her right, even closer to the building, to get a better angle to check if he had any companions. As far as she could see, there weren't any.

Now raising the Sig in a two-hand grip, she said in as commanding a voice as she could, "I am a Deputy Sheriff! Immediately but slowly raise your hands over your head!"

Taken completely by surprise, the intruder spun around to face Ro. As he was now in the full moonlight, she could see his relaxed demeanor suddenly change to hostile, and she could see a look of recognition, then surprise and then something like contempt in his eyes, maybe thinking to himself, *Hell, I can take this stupid bitch cop!*

She also saw he was wearing a bullet resistant vest and that his right hand had twitched upward toward the automatic holstered on his right hip; it looked big enough to be a .45.

Ro raised her Sig so he could see the large dark hole at the end of the barrel, and said, rather quietly, "Don't!"

He let his hand drop back to his side.

Taking a couple of steps forward, she was now maybe twelve feet from the intruder, she said with distinct purpose, "Put your hands up where I can see them, very slowly drop to your knees, then lie face down with your arms out at your sides."

Keeping the Sig's barrel pointed steadily at his face, Ro said, "Whatever you're doin' here ain't worth dying over."

He complied, sort of....

While Ro knew she should probably wait for backup, that tackling this guy single-handed was not good police procedure, she also didn't know how many more there were or if they were in the building…and if Pops was in trouble and if time was critical.

Approaching the prone figure from his right, she intended to first slide the rifle off his shoulder, next remove the pistol from his belt holster and finally cuff him. As she leaned over he made his move, suddenly flipping on his left side and swinging his foot around, trying to kick her in the head.

Always good at spotting "tells" in her judo competitions — little moves people had that telegraphed what they were going to do — out of the corner of her eye Ro had seen him ever so slightly cock his right foot back and was ready. Darting back a step, she let his foot fly past her face, then stepped in and kicked him in the groin, hard, figuring it was more humane than shooting him or cracking him on the head with her gun butt.

He doubled over in agony, grasping his crotch, a painful groan escaping his lips.

"Bad move, buddy," she said, but without sympathy. It didn't take long to disarm him and truss up his hands and feet with the two plastic flex cuffs she carried. She pulled off his ski mask — *Jesus*, she thought, *this turkey's my age!* — wadded it up, and stuffed it in his mouth. Then, patting him patronizingly on the head, she whispered in his ear, "I'll be back," grinning to herself at the irony of the "tough guy" movie reference.

Looking around, Ro spotted a stack of what looked like forms for concrete walls some twenty feet away, and dropped the perp's carbine and handgun in the shadows behind it.

Wondering how this guy's buddies might have gotten into the building, she found a fire door slightly ajar. Approaching, she could clearly see it had been forced open with some kind of pry bar.

CHAPTER TWENTY-THREE
SHOOTOUT

Wednesday, August 20, 2003, 11:04 p.m.

Just inside the fire door was a small landing. A door directly across clearly led into the main floor of the building. The front section of the shooting range building's first level housed a wide, glass-fronted entrance foyer, several classrooms, washrooms, and a small office complex. The major portion of the rear part of the building was a large, climate-controlled warehouse for old county records.

On her right a set of stairs led downward to the shooting range level, which took up the entire lower floor. She knew that here at the back of the building was the heavy backstop apparatus for bullets, the firing line being at the other end of the building, some hundred and fifty feet away.

Descending the stairs carefully, Ro again drew the Sig but kept it down at her side.

A long, narrow, tunnel-like hallway stretched out from the bottom of the stairs. Overhead were lots of pipes and what looked like heavy duty electrical conduit. On the wall to her left, which was common with the shooting range itself, were big, fan-like structures she assumed were part of the ventilation system. Small light panels spaced every twenty feet or so along the right wall provided dim, but sufficient light to see where she was going.

At the far end she could see a doorway slightly ajar, as there was a thin sliver of brightness on its left.

This is probably the same way whoever is down here got in, she guessed.

Fortunately, the hallway's concrete floor was clean swept, so her boots were virtually noiseless as she quickly moved down the hall.

When she was a little over halfway she heard a loud voice. While she couldn't make out words, it clearly sounded angry.

As she approached the doorway, she heard what sounded like someone being punched or slapped, followed by a grunt of pain. *Pops!*

Without hesitating, Ro burst through the door, kicking it open to the right, swinging her Sig up in a two-handed grip.

In less than a second she took in what was going on.

The spot in the foyer where just a few minutes ago she and Pops had been working on the Berettas was twenty feet ahead and a little to her left, the firing line directly on her left. Pops was still behind his work table, although there were only a couple of disassembled guns still laying on it; her table was cleared.

He was still in his chair, but she could see his hands were straight at his sides, yellow flex cuffs holding them down, and there was a trickle of blood on his lower lip.

Standing in front of Pops was a perp with his right fist cocked back, his face hidden by a ski mask.

You fucker! Ro thought, and had to exercise every ounce of self-restraint she could muster to keep from taking the top of his head off with a .357 slug.

A second perp, also wearing a ski mask, was standing a little back from and to the left of Pops, looking on, almost straight in

160

front of her. While his back was to her, she could see the barrel of the assault rifle he was carrying across his chest poking out to the left.

To her left a third perp, also ski masked, was positioned more or less directly behind the first perp, also looking on. However, because he was half facing her, he was the first to see her explode through the door.

Even before she had a chance to shout, "Deputy sheriff! Raise your hands!" the perp shouted, "Fuck! A cop!"

Crack-ack-ack!

Bang! Bang!

The distinctively sharp reports of Ro's Sig firing three times were so close together they sounded more like one unusually long shot. They were followed instantly by two shots from an assault rifle that sounded like a couple of cherry bombs going off. Since both the foyer and shooting range had been specially covered with sound absorbing material, there was no echo.

In an instant....

Ro saw the third perp to her left start to turn toward her and raise his assault rifle, which he was carrying across his chest hanging from a military-style shoulder harness. Because the perp outside had been wearing some kind of bullet resistant vest, she assumed these guys were as well. So, she went low with her shot, under the raised rifle, her slug slamming him right in the area of his solar plexus.

It was as if a big league hitter had whacked him across the belly with a full force home run swing. The perp doubled over, but was also driven backwards, falling on his butt and skidding some eight or ten feet down the length of the foyer, finally flopping on his side, clutching his belly and gasping for breath.

Meanwhile the second perp in front of her, surprised by his compatriot's shout, at first twisted his head right and left to see what was going on, but then started to turn counter-clockwise to bring his rifle to bear. Since he had a fraction of a second more time, his finger found the trigger on the rifle and he got two shots off. But, because Ro's shot got there at exactly the same time, his shots just punctured two holes in the foyer's ceiling tile off to Ro's left.

Her .357 slug hit where she'd aimed it, smashing into his vest just inside his left shoulder, spinning him around and throwing him face first into the heavy steel door of the closed gun vault just a couple of feet behind. He fell backward, stunned.

The third perp, in front of Pops, who was not carrying an assault rifle, instead reached for the automatic holstered on his right hip and started to turn clock-wise toward Ro. With him she had a tough choice. Because he hadn't turned very far, his vest was mostly at a right angle to her, so there was the real possibility her shot could just slide off the vest and hit Pops, who was only eighteen or twenty inches in front of him.

So, she chose to take out the perp's gun hand, literally. Her slug slammed into the middle of his right hand, which had been wrapped around the butt of the partially drawn pistol, first smashing the gun up against the side of his vest, then sending it crashing to the floor and throwing him across the table Pops had been working on. With arms and legs flailing he finally tumbled off the table and on to the floor, clutching his bloodied hand, moaning.

All three perps were down, but certainly not out.

Deciding she could use Pop's help Ro moved to her right, circling around the stunned second perp, but at the same time keeping the other two in view, until she was beside Pops.

"You okay?"

"Yeah."

Still holding the Sig in a ready position in her left hand, she reached behind her with her right, rummaged in the small pouch at her back, found the gravity knife, slid the blade out, and freed

Pops' left hand, the one closest to her. Then she handed him the knife so he could free his other hand, which he quickly did. Just as quickly he snatched-up one of the cleaned Berettas and a nearby loaded magazine, slammed it home and jacked in a round. Ro now had onsite back-up.

"The guns for this weekend are here, aren't they? That's what they were after," Ro guessed.

"Yep.... We got a couple dozen different ARs in there," Pops said, jerking his head back toward the vault door. "Some of 'em full auto, a half dozen high tech sniper rifles and a load of ammo." He shrugged. "Maybe fifty, sixty grand on the black market...."

Holstering her Sig, Ro said, "You keep an eye on these turkeys while I call in. Then I'll disarm 'em."

"You got it, Deputy."

Unhooking the microphone from her epaulet, she pressed the transmit button. "Armstrong One-Nine."

"One-Nine go!" Gwen Teague's voice was clearly anxious.

"We have four perps 10-95"—*in custody*— "I say again, four perps 10-95. One needs medical attention, but is not life threatening."

"10-04 One-Nine. Four in custody.... Will dispatch medical.... ETA on back-up two minutes, maybe less."

"10-04. We can still use the help."

"10-04 One-Nine."

Ro frowned. *Did I hear a smile in Gwen's voice? It kind of sounded like it....*

Turning to Pops, Ro said, "I'll start with him," pointing to the first perp, who was starting to catch his breath and seemed like the most immediate potential threat. "But I'll need to borrow some cuffs...all I have left are my hard cuffs."

Pops pulled two flex cuffs and another pair of steel cuffs from his belt pouch.

Being careful to not move into Pops' line of fire, she rolled the perp on his back. Because of the ski mask she could only see his eyes, which looked young to her and which were watery, as if he'd been crying. Then she saw the wet spot in his crotch.

I guess this guy's never been shot before, Ro thought, this time with just a touch of pity.

She first pulled the automatic from the holster on his hip, but had to unsnap the shoulder harness to lift free the assault rifle. Kicking them behind her, out of reach, she pushed him over on his side and bound his hands with flex cuffs, then pulled off the ski mask.

Damn, another kid!

She did the same to the second perp, who was still dazed. Without his mask he was a thirty-something with longish hair and a goatee.

After collecting all three perps' weapons and placing them on the table near Pops she said, "I'll run upstairs and let back-up in. We don't need 'em shooting out one of those nice new glass doors."

"Good idea," he said. "I can keep an eye on these guys."

As she passed the third perp on her way to the stairs at the other end of the foyer, she crouched down and said, "Raise your hand, it'll slow the bleeding," although she noticed it really wasn't bleeding that much. "Medical help's on the way." But she didn't bother to pull off his ski mask.

CHAPTER TWENTY-FOUR
ROGUE DEPUTY

Wednesday, August 20, 2003, 11:12 p.m.

The first back-up to swing into the parking lot was Deputy Mel Schreiber, followed quickly by Paul Schnell, the third shift command lieutenant. They climbed out of their cars simultaneously and headed toward Ro.

She could see an ambulance, with siren and lights going, maybe three-quarters of a mile to the west on Fairgrounds Road coming toward them. But then another set of flashing lights off to the left caught her attention; it was a slightly different light pattern than what the sheriff's cars used.

The cream-colored state police car swung into the parking lot a few seconds ahead of the ambulance. Sergeant Costas, her "friend" from the one time she'd had lunch at the King truck stop, climbed out of the state patrol car. "Can I help?"

"Sergeant Waters and I have three perps in custody downstairs. There's a fourth one cuffed behind the building," Ro said so everyone could hear, but mostly addressing the lieutenant.

"Deputy," Schnell said, turning to Schreiber, "you take the perp in the back into custody and transport him.... He's not the

165

one that needs medical, is he?" he asked Ro. She shook her head "no." Then, turning to Costas, Schnell said, "I'd appreciate it if you'd assist with that." Costas nodded assent.

"His weapons are behind a pile of concrete forms," Ro said to Schreiber and Costas.

Schreiber silently mouthed, "Okay."

Schnell, turning to Ro, said, "You and I will assist Sergeant Waters with the other perps."

When they got downstairs, Schnell glanced around, then said to Pops, "Sergeant, I see you have the situation pretty much under control."

Pops grinned at Ro, then turned to Schnell. "Uh, L.T." — he used the shorthand initials for lieutenant— "you need to know it was Deputy Delahanty here who took these characters down single-handed. They got the drop on me and had me tied up in that chair there. As far as I'm concerned, she saved my life." The pride and appreciation were unmistakable in his voice.

Schnell's eyebrows went up as he again glanced around, then turning to Ro grinned and said, "Single-handed, huh? Son-of-a-bitch...."

"Thank you, sir," Ro said quietly, flicking her eyes toward Pops, who winked.

The EMTs, with their cases of medical supplies and a collapsible gurney, arrived at the bottom of the stairs and quickly headed for the third perp, who was still holding his bloody hand. A stocky, thirty-something female, who seemed to be the senior EMT, glanced up at Schnell and pointed to the ski mask. Schnell nodded and she pulled it off, revealing a grizzled, sixtyish face. He stared at Pops.

"Jesus Christ!" Schnell muttered.

"Deputy Delahanty, meet former deputy Neal Ferris," Pops said.

"Wait a minute," Ro said, recognizing the face—although

it had been a bit younger then—from when she was a little kid and Ferris's picture on his posters and yard signs had been everywhere. "This is the guy who ran against Mark Ballard, back in what, '92?"

"Yep. Hod...," Pops used the former deputy's handle, "and I go back a long time."

As one of the EMTs started bandaging his hand, Ferris looked up at Schnell and said, "I want a lawyer. I want to make a complaint against this deputy," he jerked his head toward Ro, "for using excessive violence."

Pops laughed out loud. "Hod, you're an idiot! Excessive force.... Let's see: Three of you, all heavily armed, assault me, and actually fire on that deputy.... You face a single deputy armed with only a handgun.... And that deputy takes you down in about two seconds flat with non-lethal shots. I'd be surprised if even the sleaziest lawyer in town would buy into a lame ass defense like 'excessive force.'

"Plus, what you don't know is Deputy Delahanty here is the best shooter in Iowa. She *could have* put the slug into your ear instead of the back of your hand...easily.... So, consider yourself lucky to *still* be alive."

Then started the standard recitation of the perp's rights. "You have the right to remain silent...."

After Ro and Pops gave Schnell a short on-the-scene report—a formal debriefing and written incident reports would come later—it was decided Deputy Schreiber would ride in the ambulance with Ferris to the hospital, then either call for transport to the county jail or see him secured at the hospital. Schnell would return to the sheriff's headquarters in his car, Costas would transport one perp in his state car and Ro and Pops would transport the other two perps to the county jail in Ro's patrol car.

After loading their two prisoners in the back and slamming

the door, Pops pulled Ro aside. "Deputy, I really meant it when I said you probably saved my life. I don't think Ferris expected *me* to be there.... Maybe he thought I'd retired or something.... Anyway, he knew I'd recognized him, even with the ski mask, so I have no doubt he'd have had to shoot me so I couldn't identify him."

"Well then, Pops," she said, touching his arm, "I'm sure glad I got there in time. I know they were after the guns, but do you have any idea why?"

"Well, street talk was the cards had not been too kind to Hod recently and he owed some big money to people who don't like to be owed big money. I think he was looking for a quick fix. What I'd give a pretty penny to find out, though, is how he knew the guns got here today. Uh...," glancing at his watch, "yesterday. Besides me, only Mark Ballard and Chief Deputy Spears knew.... Maybe he had some kind of contact in Des Moines.... Hell, we'll probably never know."

CHAPTER TWENTY-FIVE
AFTERMATH

Thursday, August 21, 2003, early morning

Most of the rest of the night was taken-up with....

Number one...getting the four perps—even Ferris, his hand bandaged, had been brought to the county jail—booked and finger-printed....

Number two...turning them over to the detectives, who interviewed them to see if they could get an initial sense of their plan, but most of all to see if they could learn who they were stealing the guns for....

Although neither Ro nor Pops participated in the interviews, they watched through one-way mirrors. Ferris, of course, having been on the good guy side of the one-way mirror, and knowing how the game was played immediately "lawyered-up," refusing to answer any questions. His three henchmen seemed to be pretty clueless; having been "hired" with a promise of a share of the gun money, they claimed they'd been told their role was only to look and act scary.

"Oh, so I was just supposed to be frightened into dropping my gun and backing off when you drew down on me? Bullshit!"

Ro said to Pops as they watched.

"You sure surprised them." Pops said with a grin.

Number three…being formally debriefed by Lieutenant Schnell, and then being informally debriefed by Chief Deputy Spears and by Sheriff Ballard, who both came in to show support for their deputies….

Number four…writing their official incident reports into the computer…. For Ro, who was quite used to writing concisely and from an objective viewpoint after having done hundreds of responses to discussion questions for her online classes, it wasn't much of a chore. Of course, she double-checked what she'd written for grammar and spelling before hitting the "save" command and entering her report into the county's formal and eventually public records system.

Number five…dealing with the media…. It was uncanny how the media always found out about incidents like a shootout so quickly…maybe from monitoring police bands, maybe from a tip by a witness. The media calls — the first was from, of all places, a TV station over in Illinois — started around 2:30 a.m.

According to department policy, as the command officer on the scene Lieutenant Schnell was the only one authorized to make statements to the press, so he took all their calls. Of course, Sheriff Ballard and Chief Deputy Spears could talk to the press as well, but in a situation like this they almost always deferred to the command officer. Rather than tell the same story again and again, and even more importantly possibly getting something different in one version than in another and thus setting in motion a whole "what are the cops hiding?" speculative brouhaha, Schnell scheduled a formal news conference at 5 a.m. He even called each of the area's media, the *Lee's Landing Courier*, the Illinois-based daily paper, and all the TV stations and radio stations to make sure they knew about the time.

Of course, all four local TV news departments had a full crew on the scene, which included a cameraman and their coiffed and primped "on air" reporter. Both newspapers sent a reporter and a photographer, and the two local radio operations that still had actual news departments—most stations had been reduced to reading the headlines from the newspaper for their local news— also sent reporters. There was even "a stringer," a local freelance reporter only called in for "big" stories, from the *Des Moines Register*. Since it was a clear, warm night, and since media were not permitted inside the sheriff's department headquarters, the news conference was held on the steps of the courthouse.

Schnell first gave a statement.

At approximately 11 p.m. the night before, four perpetrators had broken into the new regional shooting range with the apparent intent to steal weapons from the gun vault. They had taken the deputy who was on the scene by surprise, subdued, and assaulted him; he named Sergeant Cyril Waters as that deputy. Another deputy, who was outside the building, noticed something suspicious and followed-up; he named Deputy Ro Delahanty as that deputy. There had been a shootout between Deputy Delahanty and three of the perpetrators; one of the perpetrators had been slightly wounded. All four were now in custody pending appearing before a judge in the morning to be charged.

While Schnell had tried to make it as matter-of-fact as possible, of course a barrage of questions was shouted at him.

No, we are not releasing the names of the perpetrators at this time.

No, I can't tell you exactly what weapons were in the vault, although it did include mostly hand guns…which, while literally true, was certainly a convenient evasion.

No, you can't interview the deputies. "You know the department's policy on that."

No, what the perpetrators will be charged with hasn't been

determined yet. You'll have to ask the county prosecutor about that in the morning.

One perpetrator received a wound to his right hand. He was taken to the hospital, treated, and released to our custody.

The deputy who was assaulted was forcibly flex-cuffed to a chair and had been punched once. He was examined by EMTs at the scene, and it was determined his only injury was a bruise to his left cheek.

A total of five shots were fired, three by Deputy Delahanty, two by one of the perps.

Sergeant Waters was on the scene because he had earlier conducted a gun safety class for some Boy Scouts, and Deputy Delahanty had assisted him. She had left to begin her regular patrol shift when she noticed suspicious activity at the rear of the shooting range building and investigated.

No, the Boy Scouts had left the scene more than an hour earlier.

Ro, Pops Waters, Sheriff Ballard and Chief Deputy Spears had all stood behind Schnell, but had said nothing during the press conference. But Ro had seen the TV cameras focus on her and on Pops, and the newspaper photographers point their long lenses at each of them as well. So, she knew their names and faces would be all over the media the next morning.

After the media left, as the entourage was filing back into the department Ballard took Ro and Pops aside. "You two had better get on the phone to your families right away. The last thing they need is to turn on the TV in a few minutes and see you were in some kind of shootout. Delahanty, why don't you use the small conference room next to my office? It'll be more private. Pops, you can use my secretary's office."

Settled into one of the eight overstuffed, executive-style chairs around what was clearly a solid wood conference table, Ro took out her cell phone and speed-dialed her parents' number.

It was close to six o'clock, so she was sure her father would be awake.

Big Mike answered after the second ring. "Hi, honey," he said, knowing it was her because his phone had recognized hers. "Anything wrong?" There was just a hint of concern in his voice; after all, she didn't often call home at this early hour.

"I just wanted to warn you and Mom, Dad, I'm gonna be on the TV news in a little while. Another deputy and I were involved in a shootout last night." Then she quickly added, "But we're okay!"

"Mother of God," Big Mike muttered. "You *promise* you're all right?"

"Absolutely, not a hair was ruffled," she said, which wasn't strictly true, but seemed to be the right thing to say. Ro then outlined what had happened, basically following Schnell's lead and trying to make it sound as routine as possible. She knew she would later need to give them the whole bloody story with all its gory details, but felt the phone was not the right venue for that.

Sounding like he had been somewhat mollified, Mike said, "You're gonna have to talk to your mother, you know. She sure as hell won't want to hear this from me! Hang on...."

After a moment, Kate's voice, clearly tense, said, "Ro?"

"Hi, Mom. Another deputy and I were in"—she almost said "a gunfight," but then caught herself and changed it to—"an incident last night. You're gonna be hearing about me on the news in a little while. There was some gunfire, so the media will probably make it sound like a big deal. We arrested the bad guys, but *we're* okay...I promise."

"You're okay?" Kate needed confirmation....

"Yes, Mom." Then she shared pretty much the same somewhat sanitized version of the incident she'd given her father.

With a promise she would come over that evening and see them—Ro smiled to herself, *I guess they still need to see me to make sure I'm really not shot full of holes* — she rang off.

Next she dialed Tuck, expecting to get his voice mail as he was not usually an early riser. But to her surprise he answered on the second ring.

"Hi!" He tried to sound light, but she could tell his voice was tight, like he already knew why she was calling.

"It's on the news already, isn't it?"

"Yep, I'm watching it right now."

"It wasn't as bad as they're probably making it sound."

Tuck's snorted laugh had a sardonic edge. "Uh, let's see.... My sister the cop trades gunfire with four bad guys with assault rifles.... No problem, just another routine day at the office."

"Only one of 'em got a couple of shots off and missed me by a mile."

"A bad guy with shitty aim...oh, thank heaven for small favors."

"Don't be a dick."

"You know me. I have to keep it light, it's how I cope."

"Yeah."

"I assume you've already called Mom and Dad."

"I just got off with them."

Then, rather unexpectedly Tuck said, "Are you proud, sis? You know you should be." This definitely was not Tuck's light side.

Ro was caught by surprise and was silent for a moment. Being "proud" of what had happened had not yet occurred to her. "Tuck, it all just happened so fast, it's like.... Well, I was just doing my job, so why's everyone making such a *thing* about it?"

"You're funny, sis. If you leaped over a tall building in a single bound like Supergirl and people expressed surprise, you'd say, 'No big deal, anyone could do that.'"

Not knowing what to say, Ro changed the subject. "I'm having dinner with them tonight. Can you come over?"

174

"Only if you promise to tell us the *whole* story."

"Y-e-s," she said with exaggerated mock resignation.

With an exchange of "love you's" they rang-off.

Next, she dialed Atti. The call seemed to take a long time to go through—*She's probably still in Europe and the cell system is trying to find her,* Ro thought—so wasn't surprised to get her friend's voice mail.

"Sorry, but you've missed your chance to talk to Atti live. You'll just have to talk to her machine instead."

"Atti, it's Ro. I thought I'd better call you instead of letting you hear about it from your parents or in an e-mail from somebody. Last night I got into an incident—oh hell, it was a gunfight—with some bad guys. But I'm *okay*! Really...."

"Holy shit! *Gunfight!*" It was Atti's live voice, pitched with excitement. Then muffled, as if she had her hand over the phone, she could be heard saying, "It's my best friend. She's a cop back home and she was in a fucking gunfight!"

Ro grinned...her friend wasn't alone. No surprise there.

"If you need me to, I can call you back later."

"Are you kidding? No way. I wanna know what happened."

Ro gave Atti the same sort of bleached account she'd given her parents.

"Oh man, just like the OK Corral."

At first Ro was going to object to the analogy...real cops didn't look for a fight like the Earp brothers seemed to, or at least as it was portrayed in the movies. But then she had to admit to her friend, the one person she had always been able to say anything to and know she wouldn't be judged, "It *was* kind of exciting."

"I always said you were a real bad ass, didn't I?"

With promises they would get together soon they rang-off.

Finally, she speed-dialed Frank's number.

"Hi, Annie Oakley," Frank said after the third ring.

Ro groaned. "Oh, it's already on the news."

"Yep, I'm watching it right now. 'Rookie cop takes down four bad guys in daring shootout,' or something along those lines."

"Rookie? Ouch."

"Um, I think the TV reporter used the word 'hero.' They're saying you saved that sergeant's life."

"Ohhh, double ouch."

"Ro, I know you're 'okay,' at least in terms of not getting shot, or I wouldn't be talking to *you* right now. But are you *okay*?"

"Yeah, yeah…. Really, I am."

There was an awkward pause, like neither one quite knew what to say next.

Filling the void, Frank said quietly, "Ro, I wouldn't like it very much if something happened to you."

Ro suddenly felt like things were getting way too heavy. *Are you proud, sis? I always said you were a real bad ass. They used the word "hero." What if something happened to you?*

"We've been so tied up with booking and paperwork and the media, I really haven't had time to even think about it," she said, avoiding the subject.

She gave Frank pretty much the same story of what had happened she'd given her parents, which seemed to satisfy him as well, at least for the moment.

At first, they talked about meeting for lunch at Papa Tony's, but then Ro changed her mind. "Could you come to my apartment, instead? I don't know if I'm ready to be a public hero quite yet."

CHAPTER TWENTY-SIX
WARRIOR

Thursday, August 21, 2003, later in the morning

By the time she got back to the bullpen at 6:45 it was crowded with deputies, some in uniform about to start their day shift, most in civilian clothes. They had rushed down to headquarters as soon as they'd heard the morning news to both maybe learn for themselves the inside scoop of what had really happened, *and* to show support for their fellow cops who'd been under fire. Ro and Pops were buttonholed repeatedly by varying groups of deputies who all wanted to hear the story, who wanted to make sure they were okay, and who just wanted to let them know "we're here."

Finally, at shortly after seven Ballard's voice boomed over the crowd. "Hey, everyone! These two deputies have had a long night and…" — pointing to a clock on the wall — "are now officially off-duty. Let's let 'em go home and get some rest."

As the crowd began to disperse, Ballard held up a finger to Pops and Ro, signaling he wanted them to wait a moment.

"I know you two are well aware of the policy," he said. "But I have to make it official any way. Beginning now you'll both be on paid administrative leave for the next few days pending

177

a shooting review and an evaluation by Doc Lewin. We can schedule the review tomorrow; we'll let you know what time. But I suspect we won't be able to get you in to see Doc Lewin before Monday at the earliest. My secretary will call you with the times."

Both Pops and Ro nodded they understood.

Even though Ro knew the policy, her first reaction was a slight frown that she was going to miss three days on duty, her regular Thursday, Friday, and Saturday night patrols.

Mistaking her look of disappointment for concern about the shooting review, Pops stepped close and said reassuringly, "Don't worry, it was a good shoot."

"I know," Ro said, then shrugged. "I'm just not sure what I'm gonna do with three days of unexpected paid vacation," putting air quotes around "vacation."

With a slightly askance look, Pops shook his head and said, "I don't believe you." Ro knew he didn't mean he thought she was lying. "I know it'll be hard," he teased, "but at least *try* to enjoy it."

"I will," she promised.

As with most law enforcement agencies, the Fort Armstrong County Sheriff's Department had a policy that whenever an officer was involved in a shooting there was an official review. The deputy or deputies involved were interviewed by a panel of senior officers, who essentially made a judgment if the use of potentially deadly force had been justified. Their finding letter went into the deputy's personnel jacket.

What's more, the deputy or deputies involved in a shooting also had to visit with Dr. Durwood Lewin, a clinical psychologist used by area law enforcement agencies. Doc Lewin's job was to determine if the officer was having any adverse psychological reactions — post traumatic stress syndrome — from the shooting that would keep him or her from returning to the job. His report also went into the personnel file.

At this point Ro was too tired to really give much thought to how she felt about the shooting review or the visit with Doc Lewin.

It took her a few more minutes to make her way out of the bullpen and to the staff door leading to the parking lot. Since the media knew that's where deputies came and went, they were waiting in force, shouting questions over one another, the TV camera's bright lights nearly blinding her.

"Give us a statement, Deputy!"

"How'd you know they were there?"

"Why'd you go in alone? Why didn't you wait for back-up?"

"Pretty lucky shooting, don't you think?"

"Why didn't you shoot to kill?"

"What'd you think when they were shooting at you?"

Trying to make her cop face even more stern than usual, Ro pushed her way through the crowd, repeating again and again as she'd been instructed, "No statement.... No statement.... No statement...."

It was a moving mob as Ro made her way toward her patrol car, in effect carrying the group with her. They'd made it about halfway across the parking lot when one of the reporters yelled, "The lieutenant's come out!"

The mob disappeared almost instantly, reappearing around Schnell near the staff door. Ro suspected he'd stepped out on purpose as a magnet to draw them off her.

"We'll have the names of the men in custody for you in about half an hour," Schnell announced to the group. Patience not being one of the press's virtues, the reporters shouted questions like, "Do any of them have a record? Are they locals? Can you tell us what kinds of guns they were carrying? Are they terrorists?"

Glad to be free of the mob, Ro took a couple of steps toward the patrol car and stumbled. Fortunately, the reporters were focused on Schnell and hadn't noticed her clumsiness…. Except it wasn't clumsiness, because she hadn't really stumbled…. Her knees were refusing to work properly…for that matter to work at all. And suddenly she felt like she wanted to throw-up.

"Weren't you scared?"

That question had been shouted by one of the female TV reporters, her voice high and soprano-like, easily carrying over everyone else's.

Ro reached the car after a few more halting steps, needing to put her hand on the roof to steady herself while she fumbled for her keys, because her fingers felt numb. Finally sliding into the car's front seat and slamming the door, she clutched the steering wheel with both hands to try and stop her shaking — *her shaking!* — and to steady her ragged breathing.

I must be crashing from last night's adrenaline rush. Or, at least it's what she tried to convince herself.

Weren't you scared?

After several tries she finally found the patrol car's ignition switch and got it started. Knowing she had to get out of the parking lot, because if the reporter's caught her sitting there they'd be on her again like jackals, she put the car in gear and let it roll forward slowly.

A thousand jumbled thoughts clawed for attention at the edges of her consciousness….

Weren't you scared?

Pretty lucky shooting, don't you think?

Consider yourself lucky to still be alive….

Lucky… Lucky? Who was lucky? Them? Me?

I was just doing my job, so why's everyone making it such a big deal?

But it is a big deal! You're only kidding yourself if you think it isn't.

Rookie cop takes down four bad guys in daring shootout.

Daring shootout…. What if the two perps on my right and left had turned at the same time? Maybe the one could have gotten his shots off a half second faster. What if the third perp hadn't been as slow on the draw?

Lucky? Who was lucky? Them? Me?

Ro's head jerked and she gasped as she suddenly had a vivid image of her body, several ugly red splotches spreading across her stomach and chest where their bullets had hit her, being slammed to the shooting range's floor because one or more of the perps had been a little quicker or she'd been a little slower.

"Oh God!" she cried aloud, closing her eyes, shaken to the core by a vision of Mark Ballard sitting in her parents' living room trying to explain to them how and why they'd lost their daughter.

Lucky? Who was lucky? Them? Me?

She'd reached the edge of the parking lot, where she would normally turn left onto Third Street to head for her apartment. At least it's what she knew she *should* do….

Rookie cop….

Lucky? Who was lucky? Them? Me?

I was just doing my job….

But instead she turned right toward Main Street, which was also U.S. Rt. 68, and which would lead her out into the county.

She knew where she *needed* to go, where she *had* to go!

Mostly on automatic pilot, forcing herself to concentrate on her driving and refusing to let any other thoughts gain traction, it took her nearly half an hour to cover the just over twenty miles from the courthouse in downtown Lee's Landing to the sprawling Witness Tree Rod and Gun Club in the rural eastern part of the county.

Witness Tree was like a second home for Ro Delahanty.

Her father had been a member for as long as she could remember, at first hunting there, but then giving it up in favor of

181

trap and skeet shooting. She'd started accompanying her father on Saturday mornings when she was ten. They would have breakfast in the club's lodge, and then she'd watch as Big Mike and his friends would plunk away at clay pigeons, competing with one another as to who was the best shot.

It didn't take Ro long—just a few months—to ask her father if she could learn to shoot like him. So, he dug out his old Stevens .410, which was the gun his father had given him to learn to shoot on, and passed it on to a third generation with pride.

Big Mike and his friends soon learned "little Ro" had, as they put it, "damn good hand eye coordination," and she quickly started knocking down clay pigeons with the best of them.

In those days, besides its two-hundred-and-fifty acre stocked fishing lake and more than fifteen hundred acres of woods and meadows for hunting, Witness Tree had a large and popular skeet range and a smaller rifle range, but no pistol range. That came when Ro was fifteen. She was one of the first to sign up for its target shooting classes, figuring it was surely a skill she needed if she really wanted to be a cop.

She'd found a used, but in good condition, Ruger Mark II .22 LR target pistol in the consignment area of the club's pro shop, and took an advance on her allowance to pay for it.

If Ro Delahanty had acquired something of a reputation around Witness Tree as a good trap and skeet shooter, she quickly gained even more renown as a fierce competitor on the pistol range, within a year walking away with medals and trophies from target matches at the local and regional level.

It was close to eight o'clock when she turned off County Road Q into the club's entrance drive. It was already past eighty degrees, and promised to be a typically hot Midwestern summer day, with the only relief a ten mile an hour western breeze.

She rolled to a stop at the entrance booth where members were supposed to check-in, and was immediately recognized and waved through, although the squad car—they were more used to seeing her in her red Explorer—raised a few curious eyebrows.

She stopped at the clubhouse. While the idea of two eggs over medium, sausage patties, hash browns, toast and a mug of strong black tea was tempting—she hadn't had anything to eat since the night before, except for a couple of donuts from a box of several dozen someone had brought in to the sheriff's headquarters—what she was really after was the key to the pistol range's small storage shed.

She drove past the skeet range—there were already half-a-dozen cars in the parking lot—to the adjacent rifle range and pistol range beyond. There were no cars in their shared parking area.

Rookie cop…. Daring shootout….

Weren't you scared?

Just doing my job….

Lucky shooting…. Who was lucky? Them? Me?

Ro climbed out of the car, opened the trunk, and retrieved two extra magazines for the Sig from her Uncle Mike's duty bag and stuffed them in her right side pants pocket. She now had five magazines for the .357, one in the weapon, two in magazine holders on her belt, and the two in her pocket. Seventy-five rounds, plus the one in the pipe.

Ro strode across the open area between the parking lot and the firing line. She was home….

She unlocked the eight-by-twelve-foot shed near the range's firing line.

When the pistol range was first built it had eight shooting positions on the firing line, with stanchions for fixed paper targets the standard twenty-five yards downrange. But two years ago, when so-called sport shooting had started gaining popularity, Witness Tree had installed a basic system of rails and springs that controlled pop-up targets in random order.

183

Ro quickly dismissed the idea of setting up a shooting sequence; after all, she'd know where the threatening targets were, so any surprise factor would be negated. Instead she simply retrieved eight standard pistol targets, a set of red flags, and a bright orange vest from a shelf in the shed.

Positioning the red flags along the firing line to warn potential shooters—even though there weren't any—that someone was downrange, Ro donned the orange vest to make sure she was highly visible, and walked across the downrange stanchions, clipping each paper target in place.

She forced herself to focus on the job at hand, blocking out anything else. Her breathing was even and steady, the jitters—or whatever the hell they had been—now seemed to be gone.

Returning to the firing line, she took down the flags, removed the vest....

Lucky shooting....

...And, stepping up to the first firing station, in one fluid motion drew the Sig, flicked off the safety with her thumb, swung the weapon up into a standard two-handed grip, and fired six rounds as fast as her finger could squeeze the trigger.

Crack-ack-ack-ack-ack-ack!

She holstered the gun, turned, and took two quick paces to the next firing position, turned, and drew the pistol....

When she was on the firing line the Sig was not something discrete from Ro.... Yes, if needed, she could remove it from its holster and hand it to someone else....

Crack-ack-ack-ack-ack-ack!

Turning, as she took the two paces to the next firing position she ejected the nearly spent magazine, pulled a fresh one from a pouch on her belt, and slammed it home. As there was still a cartridge in the pipe, she didn't need to jack in a fresh one. She holstered the weapon for a brief second, then turned and drew....

...But when Ro fired it, the gun was not *in* her hand, it was a

184

part of her hand, a part of her eye, a part of her instincts....

Crack-ack-ack-ack-ack-ack!

Being in a place, in a space where she was comfortable, confident, and in control, things became clearer, started to make sense.

Weren't you scared?

Of course, I was scared. I'd be a fool if I wasn't....

Crack-ack-ack-ack-ack-ack!

Turn, eject, new magazine, step, turn, draw, fire....

Crack-ack-ack-ack-ack-ack

...But that's the point, you don't hide from the fear, you embrace it and make it yours. You use it to focus and energize....

Crack-ack-ack-ack-ack-ack

Turn, eject, new magazine, step, draw, fire....

Crack-ack-ack-ack-ack-ack

Yes, these are only simulacrums, paper targets.... But that's exactly why you do this over and over and over...to train your eyes to see, to train your hand to react, to train your thumb to flick off the safety and another finger to curl around the trigger when your brain registers a threat....

Crack-ack-ack-ack-ack-ack

...So you don't *have to think about it...so fear isn't in control....*

It's what every warrior from time immemorial had understood.

Holstering the Sig, Ro again donned the bright orange vest, remounted the flags, and starting at the right end walked down the line of targets. As the sun was still somewhat behind the targets it was easy to see the holes her slugs had punched in each.

Forty-eight shots in eight groupings of six each....

Not a single hole was outside of the black.

Lucky shooting.... Maybe for them...not me....

CHAPTER TWENTY-SEVEN
FULL CIRCLE

Thursday, August 21, 2003, later in the morning

Calm and relaxed, having found her center, Ro walked over to a picnic bench near the shed and sat.

With the temperature now approaching ninety degrees, she swiped her forehead with a bandana pulled from her back pocket, spread out the targets and signed and dated each, then dropped them on the patrol car's passenger seat. One of the file drawers in her study held a two-inch thick pocket folder full of targets from competitions and practice sessions. Most had a witness's signature, which made them official, but she even kept some of her best targets from solo shoots...like today's.

Retrieving a still near full bottle of water from the holder next to the patrol car's front seat and a box of .357 cartridges from the duffle in the trunk, Ro went back to the picnic bench. Even though it was anything but cold, the water tasted good. Then she carefully reloaded three magazines; one went into the Sig and two went into her belt pouch. As far as she was concerned, there was no question her sidearm must *always* be at the ready. The fourth and fifth magazines went back into the duffle to be reloaded later.

Finally, she meticulously tidied up the shooting range, policing the firing line for spent cartridge casings to be thrown into a recycling bin, returning the red flags and orange vest to the shed and locking up.

It was almost ten o'clock when she swung the patrol car out of the shooting range parking lot and headed for the club's entrance, trailing a cloud of dust. As was her habit, the windows of the car were wide-open.

Ro found she was hungry; maybe it was the insistent stomach growl that literally could be heard over the rumble of the patrol car's V-8 engine. It had been what, twelve, thirteen hours since she'd had anything substantial to eat? At first the idea of stopping at the snack bar in the clubhouse near the entrance, or maybe heading over to the Truck King on I-82 to have a nice satisfying breakfast sounded good, but was quickly rejected. The last thing she needed—or wanted—right now was a lot of attention. *Hero cop takes down four bad guys in daring shootout.* The idea of having to deal with any "hero cop" stuff made her cringe. Mostly on automatic pilot, Ro drove across the county to her apartment, and at just past 10:30 backed into her accustomed spot far from other cars.

Stepping into her apartment, she half turned, locked the door behind her, and then just stood there, staring into, but not really *at*, the living room, not quite knowing what to do next.

I'm hungry, I still need to eat. I'd love to get out of this uniform— it's sweaty and sticky and smells like gunpowder—and into my sweats. I need to clean the Sig. I need to get some sleep. I should put on some music, but don't know what I feel like.

I need to sort things out.

Deciding her most immediate need was for food, Ro went into the kitchen, and though she really would have liked a big breakfast, didn't want to bother cooking for herself, so just

187

poured a glass of milk and got an energy bar from the cupboard. They helped. The dull, low blood sugar headache went away. It seemed to make it easier to think.

Intending to head down the hall to her bedroom, she turned from the small dining area off the kitchen into the living room and saw Atti's poster on the wall.

Bitch Bad Ass!

She withdrew the Sig from its holster, her hands automatically going to the two-handed grip, smoothly bringing the weapon up to near eye level in the aiming position she'd been taught six years ago when she first learned to target shoot with a pistol. Then, trying to imitate the poster, she withdrew her right hand and stuck the gun out away from her body in nearly the same aggressive, one-handed, cowboy-style firing pose the cartoon-like Ro character was using. It felt unnatural.

"Hunh!" she snorted disdainfully. "*Real* shooters don't shoot like *that*."

But despite the inauthenticity of the shooting position in the poster, Ro did not have any trouble identifying with the fierce, determined look of Atti's Bitch Bad Ass.

It was kind of exciting....

I really did want to take the top of that fucker's head off....

Re-holstering the Sig with an "oh well" sigh, she turned and headed down the hall to her den, locking the holster and gun in her gun vault, to be cleaned later. In her bedroom she stripped down, throwing the uniform into a hamper for the dry cleaners.

In the shower the Ivory smelled clean as she soaped her body with a washcloth, like she did every day, sometimes a couple of times a day. It felt comfortable, like everything was normal.

Slipping into a T-shirt and cutoff sweats – the deputy's uniform was for "out there," the comfortable sweats was for "in here" – she went back to the den and retrieved the handgun from the vault, along with an oilcloth and her cleaning kit.

Sitting down at her desk, the oilcloth stretched across the top, she dropped the Sig's magazine and jacked the slide to eject the cartridge in the barrel, then jacked the weapon twice more just to make sure it was truly empty.

Laying the now empty gun on the oilcloth, its barrel pointing to her right, she was about to disassemble it like she'd done hundreds of times before when something very weird happened. Ro suddenly had this very sexual vision of the gun, like it was this hard, dark metal penis. It aroused her, her nipples stiffening and wetness stirring between her legs.

"What the hell!" she muttered aloud, pushing herself back in her chair and staring at the gun, frowning, her head a turmoil of perplexing thoughts....

God, I really want Frank between my legs right now.

Why? I just had him two days ago.... Am I still the party girl hooked on sex and just kidding myself?

Maybe the cop stuff's all bullshit!

As far as I'm concerned, she saved my life. You're a helluva cop....

It's not *bullshit!*

Frank scares the hell out of me. Not the sex part, but getting too close.

She knew there was a double meaning; Frank getting too close to her and her getting too close to Frank. And knew it was the second part of that had frightened her more.

I want him now, *but I don't* want *to* need *him....*

Too close....

Bad ass.... Is that what I really want? What I really am? Are "bad ass" and "good cop" complimentary? Or contradictory? Or both?

I like the idea of at least the bad guys thinking I'm a "bad ass."

Can a "bad ass" really love somebody? Or be loved? Or am I just using him?

Damn you, Frank, you're not only fucking me, you're fucking with my mind.

189

Don't kid yourself, you're *the one fucking with your mind.*

Ro wrapped her left hand around the Sig's handle and held it up and out, pointing it at the wall, which was common with her bedroom and not the adjacent apartment. And she understood. *This thing* is *a phallus. It spits death or the possibility of death, just like a cock spits life or the possibility of life.* She laughed to herself. *I'll bet half the warriors in history probably couldn't wait to fuck somebody every time a battle was over, only they never talk about* that *part in the history books, do they?*

Still holding the gun, she studied it for a moment. It felt comfortable there in her hand; it felt *right*, like that's where it belonged. And an unexpected insight suddenly struck her.... *Almost exactly twelve hours ago this gun spit death or the possibility of death at several bad guys, and at least one's gun spit death or the possibility of death at me.*

I want Frank now because I need to take it full circle, to celebrate life.

Because for Ro Delahanty, sex had always been a celebration....

She laughed a biting laugh, quite unexpectedly remembering Penny Weiskopf, but then realized why.

Weiskopf had joined the Lee's Landing PD in 1992 as their first female officer. Ro remembered at the time reading an article about Weiskopf in the *Lee's Landing Courier,* and feeling encouraged because it reinforced her then new-found ambition to become a cop.

Ro met Weiskopf in 1996 when she was fourteen and did a police car ride-along as part of an eighth grade career exploration project. When Ro climbed into Weiskopf's Ford Crown Vic patrol car, she was full of enthusiasm about what it meant to be a cop, but was then deeply discouraged when Weiskopf confided to Ro all she'd been doing for four years was community service work, school presentations, and neighborhood watch recruiting and training. She had never been assigned to general patrol duty.

190

When Ro was hired by the Fort Armstrong County Sheriff's Department as a dispatcher in 2001, she was excited to find Weiskopf had become a deputy in 1997 and was indeed assigned to general patrol duty. Weiskopf became something of a role model for Ro, a role she hoped, no, *planned* on stepping into someday soon.

When Weiskopf announced a year later she was leaving the department to get married and start a family, outwardly Ro wished her all the best and really did feel that way. But at the same time, she was privately chagrined and disappointed at what she felt was Weiskopf's betrayal of her duty as a cop, and promised herself it would *never* happen to her.

While she didn't realize it at the time, Penny Weiskopf became for Ro one of those seemingly insignificant day-to-day occurrences that turns into a key piece of the puzzle that later helps make sense of things. But she realized it now…Ro closed her eyes and breathed a sigh of relief.

I am a cop; I am a warrior; I cannot let that happen to me; I won't allow *that to happen to me!*

Still holding the Sig, she contemplated it for a moment, then returned it to the vault to be cleaned later.

Going back to the bedroom, she carried Peter into the den and placed him in the recliner, explaining, "Frank's coming over." His crooked smile reassured her he understood. She walked down the hall and unlocked the door to her apartment.

Returning to the bedroom, she undressed, plumped-up some pillows, and sat back against the headboard, naked…. And waited….

*I know I'm using you, Frank. I'm sorry I am only able to let you in so far…*then giggled at the unintentional double entendre, "let you *in." We'll see if that can be enough for you.*

The fairness side of Ro knew she should eventually share these feelings with Frank. *Just not today…*

191

Looking down at her naked body, Ro liked what she saw. Full, but not grotesquely large breasts, and perky — that's what one lover had once called them — nipples; a flat belly ending in a patch of mysterious red gold fur seeming to invite exploration; and long, sinewy legs.

…today I just need you to celebrate this body, to celebrate being alive *with me.*

CHAPTER TWENTY-EIGHT
RO'S HANDLE

Friday, September 12, 2003, 8:50 a.m.

It all made sense now. Ro and a county jailer—the name
badge on his tan uniform said *C. Mendoza*—were standing in
front of a large, easel-mounted architectural rendering of the
new law enforcement campus. Ro, along with maybe half the
other deputies there, was also in uniform, even though she was
officially off-duty.

Everyone knew what the shooting range—officially called the
Regional Firearms Facility—looked like because it was already
built; and everyone had seen drawings of the new regional jail,
because it was now under construction. But not until today had
anyone seen what the new sheriff's headquarters, positioned
between the two other buildings, was going to look like.

Perhaps because Ro's friend Atti was a graphic artist and
some of her sensitivity to how things were presented visually
had rubbed off, Ro nodded in appreciation at how the architects
had handled the diversity of the three buildings that would
eventually stand cheek by jowl. Rather than try to impose some
sort of incompatible unifying theme, they had instead chosen to

193

embrace that each was a different building with a different size and a different purpose.

The shooting range was on the right. It was the smallest building, with only a single floor above ground. It had a mostly glass front, a wide entrance foyer, and a set of canopy-covered doors in the center. It was set back from the street, with a small parking area in front joining a much larger lot on its right.

At three stories, the jail, on the far left, was the largest building in the complex. There was no helping it ended up with a vaguely fortress-like appearance...after all, it *was* a jail. It, too, had a canopy covered entrance that looked out on a small parking area in front, but with a much larger lot wrapped around to the left.

Even though it wasn't the biggest building — it had only two floors — the new sheriff's headquarters that stood between was clearly the dominant structure. It was slightly forward of its neighbors, and instead of any parking in front there was a park-like courtyard reaching all the way out to the street. It, too, had a canopy covered entranceway, but this canopy was somehow just a bit fancier, a bit more imposing than the other two.

Next to the street, across almost the entire width of the three buildings, was a four-foot high wall with "Fort Armstrong County Regional Law Enforcement Campus" etched into it in two-foot high letters. Ground mounted floodlights were clearly meant to illuminate the sign at night.

"Pretty cool, huh?" said C. Mendoza, knowing in another year or so that's where he'd be working.

"Sure is," agreed Ro.

Deputy Delahanty and jailer Mendoza were only two of close to sixty people in one of the larger meeting rooms of The Captain's Hotel in downtown Lee's Landing. The sheriff's department — which included not only the deputies and support staff, but the county jail staff and courthouse bailiffs and security personnel — years ago had outgrown any of the courthouse's spaces to house the quarterly all-department meetings.

There were nine rows of eight chairs each, with a wide aisle up each side. In front was a slightly raised dais with a lectern in the center, an American flag on the right, a county flag on the left. Overhead was a big screen intended for presentations, now displaying a huge rendition of the sheriff's department five-pointed star, with "For Armstrong County Sheriff's Department" in an arc on top and "Established in 1838 Iowa's Oldest Law Enforcement Agency" across the bottom.

At the back were tables with several coffee pots and platters of noticeably depleted pastries and muffins.

Sheriff Mark Ballard mounted the stage. As always, he was wearing his uniform, including a sidearm. It was an exact duplicate of his deputy's uniforms, except on each chocolate brown shoulder epaulet it said "Sheriff" in gold letters. In his late fifties, a fair amount of gray appearing at his temples, Ballard had a longish, dignified look; at six-four, he was the tallest one in the room.

Two other people mounted the stage, but stood to each side of and slightly behind Ballard. One was also uniformed and armed; also in his late 50s, he was shorter and beginning to thicken in the middle. He was Major John Spears, the Chief Deputy and Ballard's second in command. The other was a forty-something woman in a mannish dark pants suit, her medium blonde hair pulled back in a conservative bouffant, glasses hanging from a chain around her neck. However, her kindly eyes and half-smile gave her an open, accessible look. She was Jacklyn Zahn, the sheriff department's administrative director. In effect, she was the department's CFO to Spears' COO.

The appearance of the sheriff at the lectern was enough for most of the people to end conversations and find chairs. With a deep and booming, "Shall we get started," Ballard quickly got everyone else quieted down and seated.

Getting the obligatory "thank you" to everyone for taking time from their busy schedules to attend out of the way — the irony was that attendance at the quarterly meetings was mandatory — Ballard got down to business. He pressed a button on a small remote he was holding and the sheriff's logo on the big screen was replaced by a giant version of the architect's drawing Ro had been studying.

"I'm pleased to share with you today we have received final approval of the plans for the new sheriff's headquarters," he said. "The county will start taking bids after the first of the year, and we expect construction to begin next spring. If everything goes according to schedule, our building and the new county jail should be done at about the same time, in the spring or summer of 2005."

A smattering of applause was quieted when Ballard raised his hand. "Unfortunately," he said, "politics had to rear its ugly head. The price of getting final approval for the plans was that Jacklyn," he nodded toward the woman, "and I will still have our main offices in the courthouse instead of at the campus. It seems the supervisors and the county administrator want to be able to 'reach out and touch' us," he said, paraphrasing the old AT&T ad slogan, whenever they have a question.

"*However*," he added, emphasizing it by raising his voice, "just because my 'main office' will supposedly be downtown, it doesn't mean I'll be chained to it. You'll still be seeing plenty of me, maybe even more than you'd like, out on Fairgrounds Road."

More laughter and applause.

After a brief pause, Ballard pressed the remote button again and a version of his last campaign poster — it said "Re-elect Mark Ballard Sheriff" in bold dark letters, with a five-pointed sheriff's star in gold silhouette behind — appeared on the screen. There was an audible intake of breath from the audience.

"*And*, in that vein," Ballard said with a grin, "since I keep hearing no one else seems to want this job" — rumors had been circulating in the law enforcement community that no one had the guts to run against him — "I guess I'll just have to announce for a fourth term."

That brought a round of enthusiastic laughter and applause.

"I wanted all of you in the department to be the *first* to know," he said, adding, "we'll be meeting with the press later this morning to make it official for everyone else."

The sheriff's department logo re-appeared on the screen.

"Now, for *my* favorite part of these meetings," Ballard said. "Recognizing our people."

He called up to the front Deputies Nick DeGrau and Joe Spanno, who each received their corporal's stripes, and then Deputy Tom Pease, who got his sergeant's stripes. Then he called up Deputy Calvin Flowers, who got his ten-year pin, and Deputy Harry Gould, a detective, who received his twenty-year pin.

Although they were generically called "pins," only the first was a pin worn on the flap of the right breast pocket of a deputy's dress uniform just below the name badge. Any subsequent "pins" were hung from the first pin by small rings, ladder-like. Pins were awarded for a variety of accomplishments, including reaching major service anniversaries, achieving a specialty designation, like becoming a member of the department's SWAT team, and for any outstanding accomplishment as determined by the sheriff.

"Sergeant Waters, please come forward," Ballard called.

Pops, in uniform, made his way down the right hand aisle to the dais, climbing up next to Ballard.

Where Ballard always addressed his officers as "deputy," this time he more familiarly used Pops' handle. "Pops, Jacklyn's people checked the department's records very carefully for me, and as far as we can tell," he held out one of the small pins, "*you* are the first Fort Armstrong deputy ever to receive a forty-year pin. Congratulations."

197

He handed the pin to Pops and they shook hands. There was lots of cheering and applause.

As Pops turned to leave the dais, Ballard commanded, but with an easy tone, "Stand fast, Deputy! Just handing you another anniversary pin is far too ordinary. Pops, you have dedicated your entire adult life to this department, and that's *anything* but ordinary. What's more, I don't think there's a deputy on the force you haven't trained. As far as I'm concerned, *you* are the one person who is most responsible for the professionalism and excellence of this department.

"So, Pops, as a way for me—for *us!*—to recognize and most importantly *honor* your service to this department, as sheriff I am promoting you to the honorary rank of *Senior* Sergeant Cyril Waters. As such, you can add this star," he handed Pops a small gold star, "above those stripes on your sleeve." With a grin, Ballard added, "While it doesn't come with any extra pay, Pops, it certainly *does* come with the entire department's respect and appreciation."

Ballard then stepped back to let Pops be "the star" and started a round of applause, which was quickly taken up, along with lots of whistles and bravos, by everyone.

When Pops finally left the dais Ballard again stepped to the lectern and said, "Will Deputy Delahanty please come forward?"

Incongruously, the first thought passing through Ro's mind as she made her way forward was, *Shit, I'm sure glad I wore my uniform instead of a T-shirt and shorts!*

She found it hard to breathe standing next to the sheriff and in front of the entire department, all looking at her.

"Deputy," Ballard said, looking at Ro, his voice suddenly lower and more serious, "you faced a situation few police officers ever encounter...*four* well-armed perpetrators who had already assaulted and incapacitated a fellow deputy, who drew down on you, and who fired on you.... Where you would have been entirely justified in using lethal force in such a dangerous situation"—her copy of the official shooting review letter she'd received several days ago had said pretty much that same thing— "instead you returned fire with restraint, and I might add with uncanny accuracy, and were able to disarm all four perps and take them into custody without serious injury. Deputy Delahanty, I'm proud to present to you this commendation for uncommon valor."

He handed Ro a gold colored pin—all the others had been silver—she later found simply said "Valor," *and* that she also later learned was the department's highest commendation.

With a smile, Ballard stepped forward and offered his hand, adding, "Deputy Delahanty, you're one helluva cop! I am *really* proud to have you in my department."

Pops and Eddy Rivera were the first on their feet leading the applause, but everyone else quickly followed. Meanwhile, Ro stood at attention on the stage smiling, maybe for once in her life truly enjoying the attention.

After Ro left the dais, Ballard ended the meeting by simply calling out, "Thanks everyone."

Two groups quickly formed around Ro and Pops, with people moving back and forth between them to offer congratulations, to clap them on the back, or shake their hand.

Someone in the group of nearly a dozen around Ro— later they figured out it was Gary Stahl, a three to eleven shift deputy—said, more to everyone in general than to Ro, "You know, Delahanty's just like that cool, kick ass chick in the *Alien* movies.... What's her name?"

It was Sergeant Al Vanzante, a detective, who chimed in, "I think it was Ripley! Yeah, Ripley...."

Eddy Rivera simply said, nodding his head, "Ripley.... Ripley.... I like that...."

Ro's eyes met Rivera's and she opened her mouth to say

something, except she couldn't figure out what to say. Instead, she grinned at her friend, because she understood what was happening. She was getting her handle! And if she didn't grin she'd probably lose it...again....

"Yeah," Rivera said, louder this time, now making sure everyone could hear. "Ripley! Yeah, I like that!"

And that was all it took. By the following Monday everyone in the department knew Deputy Ro Delahanty's handle was "Ripley."

But what all of the deputies there — except Rivera, who along with his girlfriend Gloria had been to Ro's apartment — didn't know was the irony that posters for Ro's three favorite movies hung on a wall in her study: *The Godfather*, which she considered the finest American movie ever made, *Citizen Kane* and *Casablanca* notwithstanding; *L.A. Confidential*, with Russell Crowe and Guy Pearce, a modern noir film about two cops who lose their way, but ultimately find redemption; and *Aliens*, James Cameron's second installment of the *Alien* series, precisely *because* Sigourney Weaver played such a "kick ass chick."

But what *Ro* didn't know was that there was a double irony involved in getting her deputy's handle.

Within a few days of her becoming a deputy, Pops Waters had overhead two deputies refer to her as "Three B's." When he asked them what "Three B's" stood for, he was told it was "boots, buckles and boobs." Pops then gently yet firmly laid an arm across each deputy's shoulder, and pulling them in close said very quietly, "If I *ever* hear that handle again, you two will be the *first ones* I'll see get written-up for sexual harassment."

Then he looked each deputy in the eye with raised eyebrows, not having to say, "Got it?"

Both nodded.

CHAPTER TWENTY-NINE: EPILOGUE
"AT MY BACK...."

Wednesday, September 17, 2003, 2:35 a.m.

Ro was eastbound on Duet Road, quite typically for Fort Armstrong County at this time of year flanked by stubbly, just harvested cornfields on one side and lush bean fields nearly ready for picking on the other. It was unusually warm and humid for a mid-September night, and the clouds seemed to be trying to build up to do something later.

While Duet Road itself was rather nondescript as county roads go, at this end it slowly rose toward County Road G and Rickett's Ridge, which was one of Ro's favorite spots in the county. She was pretty sure Rickett's Ridge was a mound of gravel and boulders left over from some long gone glacier, and knew it was the highest point in the county because she had once looked it up on a topographic map at the library.

Ro liked it because there was a spot just a few hundred yards north of where Duet Road intersected with G from which there was a commanding view to both the east and the west. It was a spectacular place to watch sunsets to the west, which she rarely got to see because it was always dark at the beginning of her regular shift, or to revel in splendid easterly sunrises, which she had to resist the temptation to do every morning because she didn't want to establish too much of a pattern in her patrol routes. At this time of night, though, she could see all the way to U.S. 68, six miles to the east, and Interstate 82, some seven miles off to her right, with their endless streams of tiny white headlights and even tinier red taillights crawling along.

Her radio crackled. "Armstrong Two-Six" — it was Rick Matero — "to Armstrong One-Nine, go to tac two."

Ro picked up her microphone, pressed transmit, and said, "10-04 Two-Six."

On tac two Matero asked, "One-Nine, what's your 10-20?" — *location.*

When Ro told him, Matero said via the radio, "10-25" — *meet in person* — "at the Pinky." She knew it meant the entrance to the county's Pincatauwee Forest Preserve off Bell's Lake Road, maybe some six or seven miles to her north and east.

"10-04 Two-Six. 10-77" — *estimated time of arrival* — "fifteen" — *fifteen minutes.*

"10-04 One-Nine."

Not quite fifteen minutes later the two black and whites were parked driver's door to driver's door, so Ro and Matero were face-to-face maybe two feet apart. Two security lamps on tall poles to each side of the park entrance threw a bright circle of yellowish light over the cars.

"Hey, Ripley," Matero said.

"Cowboy," Ro said, by way of greeting. "What's up?"

While it was not unusual for deputies to "10-25," there was generally a reason.

Where typically Matero's expression was open and friendly, Ro could see a hint of embarrassment. "Well," he began, a little tentatively. "I wanted to tell you a story.... And then see if maybe I could talk you into joining us for lunch at the King."

When Ro's eyebrow went up with some disdain, Matero quickly raised his hand in a kind of peace gesture.

"Ripley, I think you might really like this story, 'cause Foley pretty well got ripped a new asshole." Foley was the principal, though not entirely the only, reason Ro had avoided lunches at the King over the last couple of months.

Her curiosity piqued, she said, "Okaaay...."

"Last Friday night" — it was not lost on her it was the same night as the sheriff's all-department meeting where she'd acquired her handle — "Cue was telling everyone at the table about your pin, and Foley started in that was all crap, Waters had probably been the one to take down the bad guys and they were just trying to make the...." He paused, suddenly not knowing what to say.

"Cunt cop?" Ro offered.

Matero rolled his eyes and nodded agreement, then skipped ahead in the story. "...look good."

There was a part of Ro that wanted to destroy Foley's manhood with a well-placed kick, but there was also a part of her that thought, *So, what else is new*, meaning there would always be sexist pigs like Foley in the world.

Seeing the brief flash of anger cross Ro's face, Matero quickly added, "Hang on...hang on.... I told you you'd like this story. Anyway, the statey, Sergeant Costas, you know him, was there, and so was his lieutenant, Doug Payne. Does *that* name ring a bell?"

"I remember him; we met at the Iowa Shooter's match last spring...he was one of the finalists."

"Yeah. Well, every month or so Payne does a ride around with Costas, and usually stops at the King for lunch. He sure remembers *you*.... When Foley started in with his bullshit, Payne told him to shut the hell up because he didn't know what he was talking about. Payne told Foley he'd shot against you last spring. He explained how targets would suddenly pop up out of nowhere, and that you never knew if it was going to be a civvy or a bad guy, sometimes one right after the other, or even both at the same time. He said everybody—everybody *except you!*—drew down on civvies at least once, which loses points. And he said almost everybody, including himself, drilled at least one civvy, for which you lose *big* points—*except you!*

"Now I'm quoting here," Matero said, leaning forward. "Payne got eye to eye with Foley. 'Delahanty's the coolest shooter I've ever seen. If I knew I was going into a gunfight, I'd take *her* at my back over everyone at this table *put together!*"

Matero raised his eyebrows and cocked his head a little to the left, as if to say, "So, what do you think of my story?"

Ro couldn't help but smile at the image of Payne eyeball-to-eyeball with Foley, and Foley maybe kind of cowering into himself with shame.

"That *is* a good story, Cowboy," she admitted.

"I thought you'd like it.... I already talked to Buzz...." Sergeant Ray "Buzz" Horton was one of several African-American deputies. "He'll take swing man tonight."

Ro, who had been resting her left elbow on the driver's side window, held out her arm toward Matero, so it was almost in his face. "Well, why don't you just twist my arm while you're at it?" she said.

Grinning, Matero took her wrist and did gently twist it, "There, consider your arm twisted."

The truth was Ro *did* miss the potential camaraderie with fellow cops at the lunches, and *did* have to concede her dodging them so obstinately had maybe been just a little childish.

Looking across at Matero with an "Okay, here goes" expression, she picked up her microphone, pressed the transmit key, and said, "Armstrong One-Nine, 10-7 at the King"—*out of service for lunch at the Truck King.*

"10-04 One-Nine," Gwen Teague acknowledged, with just a

204

hint of a smile in her voice.

The usual suspects were all there when she and Matero got to the truck stop a few minutes later: Cue from the sheriff's department, Foley and Liggett from the Lee's Landing PD, and Costas.

As they approached the "Police Only" table, Cue pushed his chair back, stood up, and put his hand on the empty chair next to his. "Ripley…," he said.

The End

Here is an exciting chapter from
the next Ro Delahanty novel

The Berlin Riddle
By Dave Lager

10-80 — PURSUIT IN PROGRESS

Wednesday, March 10, 2004

1:05:30 a.m. - The big, 4.6-liter V-8 under One-Nine's hood had no trouble climbing up the grade on Forest Preserve Road out of the Pinky Valley. It was a clear chilly night with brisk south winds that made it feel ten degrees colder. Even so, as was her habit, Ro still had her windows partially down so she could hear what was going on around her. A bright, three-fourths moon had just set.

Her plan was to turn west on Upper Bluff Road toward Peacock, a town of about twelve hundred. A few nights ago, she'd patrolled the half-dozen residential streets on the south side of town; tonight she thought she'd cover the northern half.

In her seven months of third shift patrols she'd learned that even in the middle of the night there always seemed to be someone about…a late night insomniac out for a stroll, a car off to or returning from an errand, someone standing on a porch smoking a cigarette. Ro believed that as these folks depended on the Fort Armstrong County Sheriff's Department for their protection, she should be regularly visible not only on the county's main roads, but also its gravel back roads and small town side streets.

1:07 a.m. - "Armstrong One-Nine." It was her friend Gwen Teague's baritone, the regular dogwatch dispatcher.

"One-Nine," Ro acknowledged.

"One-Nine, we have an LLPD 10-80 involving two vehicles"—*a Lee's Landing Police Department officer has a pursuit in progress involving two different vehicles*— "entering county jurisdiction westbound on County P."

County Road P was a paved east-west road that was an extension of Crosstown Road, a main commercial thoroughfare in the city of Lee's Landing. The LLPD officer was coming into her primary patrol area, the western part of Fort Armstrong County.

The pursuit was about a third of the way up the county from the south, while she was at its northern edge, at least ten or eleven miles away.

"LLPD," Teague continued, "says the lead vehicle is an older white Chevy pickup; the second vehicle is a dark colored Pontiac SunFire."

"Huh, a coyote chasin' a buffalo," Ro muttered to herself, picturing the little car figuratively nipping at the heels of the big pickup. Aloud she radioed back to Teague, "10-04. My 10-20"—*location*— "westbound on Upper Bluff Road a half-mile west of Forest Preserve Road. 10-76"—*en route*— "to intercept."

Ro activated the red-blue strobe light bar on the patrol car's roof, but not the siren, as she was not in actual hot pursuit. Making sure her hands were in the ten-two position on the steering wheel, she depressed the accelerator slowly but steadily, remembering her police academy instructor's dictum that "squealing tires are for phony TV cops, not *real* cops," and leveled her speed out at about fifty-five, thinking it would be all too easy to go charging around the county at high speeds and completely overshoot the pursuit.

Upper Bluff Road was a straight, mostly flat east-west two-lane blacktop that ran the full width of the county. On its north, her right, was the bluff dropping down to the Pincatauwee River valley; steep and heavily wooded, at best farmers used it for pasture. On the south, her left, stretched dozens of rolling

208

farmsteads, this time of night each one a small island of light in otherwise broad, pitch-dark fields.

She was two miles east of Peacock.

1:09 a.m. - "Armstrong One-Nine." It was Teague.

"One-Nine."

"One-Nine, LLPD says the pursuit has passed the Illowa Freeway interchange and turned right at a four-way stop."

"That's County V," Ro confirmed, "they're northbound."

Okay, they're coming in my direction, she thought.

1:11:30 a.m. - "Armstrong One-Nine."

"One-Nine."

"One-Nine, pursuit has turned left by a big white tank. LLPD doesn't know the county. Can you ID his 10-20?"

Ro knew the location well: The tank contained anhydrous ammonia—fertilizer—that serviced the thousands of acres of corn fields in the surrounding area.

"Dispatch, they're zigzagging across the county. They've turned west on Fairly Road, toward Fourth."

"10-04. 10-12"—*standby.* Teague was going to relay the information to the LLPD.

Fourth was a small town of about five hundred. Its claim to fame was its two churches, one a more than hundred-year old red brick Presbyterian church, the other a new, very contemporary Catholic church, outnumbered the town's one tavern.

1:13 a.m. - "Armstrong One-Nine," Ro said into her mic.

"One-Nine go," Teague acknowledged.

"Can you get an ID on the LLPD officer for me?"

After a moment Teague came back. "Foley."

Ro chuckled. Foley was one of the regulars at the cop's table at the always-open Truck King gas station-restaurant where Lee's Landing officers, sheriff's deputies and state patrol troopers liked to have their middle-of-shift lunch. Ro didn't much like Foley because of his "I'm God's gift to women" opinion of himself. The best one could say was they had an arm's length relationship.

As she slowed down approaching Peacock from the east, her neighborhood patrol plan forsaken, Ro figured she could either turn south onto County Road G at the main intersection in town, which would lead her in the direction of the chase, or stay on Upper Bluff Road to where it met County Line Road some six miles west of Peacock, and then turn south.

Fifty-fifty chance of intercepting them either way, she thought. For some reason her instincts said to continue through Peacock and stay westbound on Upper Bluff Road. Ro always paid attention to her instincts.

1:15 a.m. - Ro's radio crackled. "Armstrong One-Nine."

"One-Nine," she acknowledged.

"LLPD says pursuit has turned right at a four-way stop in Fourth, by two big churches."

"They're northbound on Flint Road," Ro answered.

"10-04," Gwen said. "10-12 while I relay."

Flint was a very hilly, mostly north-south road that crossed the headwaters of several creeks. The pursuit was now near the western edge of the county; her decision to keep going west on Upper Bluff Road toward County Line Road turned out to have been a good one.

This is almost like a chess game, Ro thought, *only it's perps and patrol cars jockeying for position on a county map instead of chessmen on a chessboard.*

Ro did wonder, though, what kind of "chase" this would turn out to be; probably just a couple of DUIs — *driving under the influence* — with lead feet. She'd had maybe a half-dozen "chases" so far, all speeders, but no hot pursuits of fleeing bad guys... yet....

1:17 a.m. - "Armstrong One-Nine."

"One-Nine."

"Prepare to receive 10-21."

Once upon a time a 10-21 meant to call the station on a land line; now it meant use your cell phone. It also meant information would be exchanged they didn't want out over the air for anyone with a monitor to hear. It was not unusual to get a 10-21 call, but neither was it common.

After a few seconds, the phone in a small pouch on her kit belt rang. She pulled it out, clicked on the speaker phone function, and slid it into a small bracket on the dashboard, glad her siren wasn't going as it always drowned out even the loudest speaker phone setting.

"I'm here," Ro said to the phone.

"LLPD just relayed Foley was able to get a license number on the SunFire. It's registered to a Starla Jasper, twenty-one, at an address in Lee's Landing close to where he started his pursuit. LLPD also found a ten-year old Chevy pickup registered to a Cliff Mars, thirty-two, at the same address. And get this: There've been a half-dozen 10-16" — *domestic disturbance* — "calls at that address in the last eighteen months."

"Mmm, seems like Starla and Cliff aren't getting along too well," Ro said. *A lover's spat*, she thought.

There was a few seconds pause; Ro wondered if the call had been dropped.

Then Teague came back. "Standby, One-Nine."

After half-a-minute….

1:18 a.m. - Still on the cell, Teague said, a little anxiously, "One-Nine we've got a 187." — *homicide* — "Repeat, a 187."

Uh oh, the "spat" seems to have gotten serious….

"LLPD reports right after Foley started his pursuit they got a call from a neighbor to the address that there'd been gunfire. LLPD sent a car and found a deceased female, naked, in one of the bedrooms, shot twice, with additional bullet holes in the wall and bed. The neighbor who called said he'd heard shots and looked out his window to see what was going on, and saw Mr. Mars

211

jump through a side window only wearing some underwear. Someone from inside, he assumes it was Ms. Jasper, but did not see her, fired several more shots at Mr. Mars, a couple of which hit the side of the neighbor's house. Then he heard squealing tires and saw the truck being chased by the SunFire."

Mmm, spray'n'pray, Ro thought to herself, assessing Ms. Jasper's shooting skills as the kind who just keeps pulling the trigger in the hope of hitting something.

"Dispatch, can you find out if the LLPD has a count on how many shots were fired and what the caliber might be?"

"Will do. Stand by...."

On her patrols Ro had established a regular habit of always looking around at her surroundings...front, right, left, rearview side mirrors. Now just west of Peacock on Upper Bluff Road, out of the corner of her eye she caught movement in the edge of the trees to her right. First one deer, quickly followed by another, a doe and her fawn, bolted into the road maybe thirty yards directly ahead.

"Oh, shit!" she said out loud, forgetting for the moment the speaker phone was still live.

"What?" Teague demanded.

Hitting one or both deer at her speed, now over sixty-five miles an hour, would certainly kill the deer and destroy her patrol car, putting her out of the chase. But Ro also knew just slamming on the brakes would likely put her in an out-of-control fishtail that could either end up sideswiping one or both deer, or getting the car stuck in a deeply furrowed corn field, again putting her out of the chase. Instead Ro lifted her foot from the gas pedal, allowing the car to slow at its own pace, and eased to the right, putting its right side wheels on the very edge of the gravel swath next to the pavement. The tips of several low branches whipped the right side of the patrol car.

But she missed the deer by inches. It was almost as if the

212

fawn's white tail could have swooshed across her left side window.

"Almost hit a deer," she breathlessly responded to Teague. "But I'm okay."

"Oh man! Wouldn't wanna bang up that pretty patrol car of yours."

"Sure wouldn't," Ro said aloud, then patting the dashboard thought to herself, *Good job, Mr. Pete.* She had nicknamed the squad car, a black and white Ford Crown Vic, after her childhood teddy bear, a big black and white panda, Peter Panda.

1:22 a.m. - The radio crackled. "Armstrong One-Nine."

"One-Nine."

"The pursuit has turned left from Flint onto a gravel road," Teague said.

"It's probably Giddymint Creek Road; it's the only gravel road in the area. They're going west, just a mile from County Line Road. My 10-20 is just turning south onto County Line. I'm maybe seven or eight miles north heading in their direction."

"10-04."

County Line Road was a four-lane highway literally straddling the line between Fort Armstrong County and Makuakeeta County to the west. The intersection the pursuit was approaching with County Line Road was a T; they either had to turn north, in her direction, or south. Since south would take them back in the direction of Lee's Landing, Ro was pretty sure they'd turn right, toward her.

Not quite five miles south of her, between her and the pursuit, was a four-way stop. Montgomery Road went east (to her left, their right) back into Fort Armstrong County toward the small town of Montgomery; Good Road headed west (to her right, their left) into Makuakeeta County.

1:23 a.m. - "Armstrong One-Nine," Ro said into her radio.

"One-Nine go."

"I am about seven miles from the pursuit and five miles from the Montgomery-Good Road four-way."

"10-04. Prepare to receive a 10-21."

1:23:30 a.m. - Ro's cell phone rang. "I'm here," she answered.

"LLPD says it looks like a total of five shots in the house, two in the body, three in the bed or the wall behind the bed; then four more shots into the yard and neighbor's house, presumably at Mr. Mars. They said it looks like a nine mill" — *millimeter.*

"Okay, nine shots, nine mill. Thanks."

An automatic for sure, Ro thought. *If it's a compact, she's empty or close to it. If it's a full-size, maybe seven or eight rounds left.*

1:24 a.m. - "One-Nine."

Ro replied, "One-Nine."

"Pursuit has turned north on County Line Road. They're headed straight for you."

"10-04."

Ro finally hit her siren and depressed the accelerator, swiftly moving up to seventy. Checking all around, there were no other cars on the road she could see. Her intention was to try to reach the Montgomery-Good Road four-way at roughly the same time as the chase and proceed as circumstances dictated, as was the custom deferring to the LLPD car that had been in continuous hot pursuit.

But now knowing at least one of the perps—if there was a dead body involved, that made one or both "perpetrators"—was possibly armed and appeared willing to use the weapon, she thought, *This could get real ugly.*

1:25:30 a.m. - Ro could now see three sets of headlights coming toward her. The first set seemed brighter, probably the truck. Possibly due to its larger engine, the truck had opened-up a gap of maybe sixty or seventy yards ahead of the second vehicle, the SunFire. Foley's patrol car, with its alternating red and blue strobes, looked to be twenty-five yards behind the Pontiac.

It was clear they would get to the four-way stop ahead of her.

Glancing off to her right, she spotted another set of red-blue strobes approaching on Good Road, perhaps still a mile or so off. With the possibility the pursuit might leave the county, both the Makuakeeta Sheriff and the Iowa State Police had probably been notified: the approaching car would be one of the two.

Ro also knew there was likely at least one other Fort Armstrong deputy on the way as back-up.

Grinning to herself, she muttered aloud, "This thing is turning into quite a cop circus."

1:27 a.m. - Suddenly the truck's headlights, maybe two-hundred-and-fifty yards ahead, seemed to dip and then swing from side-to-side.

He's slammed on the brakes and is fishtailing, Ro thought. *He's getting ready to turn.*

The lights then swung to her left, the driver's right.

"Armstrong One-Nine," Ro radioed in.

"One-Nine go."

"Pursuit is headed east on Montgomery Road."

"10-04. Be advised, Armstrong One-Four is 10-76" — *en route* — "northbound on Flint Road, passing Giddymint Creek."

"10-04."

One-Four was Sergeant Ray Horton, one of three African-American deputies, filling in for the regular third shift deputy, Gil Stern, who had the night off.

It meant he was a maybe three miles south of them.

Montgomery was a community of twenty-four hundred with its own four-man full-time police force. It was about four miles east of County Line Road. They were not quite a mile from County Line Road when Ro wondered if the Montgomery PD had been notified. She was just reaching for her mic to check with dispatch when the truck suddenly took a right turn.

1:29:30 a.m. - "Armstrong," Ro called in.

215

"One-Nine go."

"Pursuit has turned south from Montgomery Road and is southbound on Flint Road."

"10-04."

For all intents and purposes the fleeing vehicles had now doubled back, although Ro doubted whoever was driving the truck understood that.

With Armstrong One-Four northbound on the opposite side of the pursuit—in fact, Ro could now see his red-blue flasher approaching, which meant the truck probably could as well—and Foley and Ro behind, the fleeing vehicles were now caught, pincer-like.

1:31 a.m. - "Oh my god," Ro muttered out loud, again grabbing for her mic....

"Armstrong One Nine."

"One-Nine go."

"Pursuit has turned east onto Old Quarry Road."

There was a brief pause, almost as if Teague couldn't quite believe what she'd heard.

"Old Quarry Road, 10-04," she finally confirmed.

Like Ro, Teague knew perfectly well Old Quarry Road was a very rough gravel road that ran for not quite a mile to a dead end at a pond surrounded by high rock bluffs. The old quarry was popular with young people for keggers. In fact, Ro made it a habit to several times a week, especially on Friday and Saturday nights between midnight and two o'clock, check the area. More than a few times she had shooed away partiers. She certainly hoped there were none tonight.

The fleeing vehicles had nowhere to go; they were trapped.

1:32 a.m. - The truck skidded to a stop right at the edge of the pond, slewing sideways, so the driver's side was facing them, its headlights illuminating a thirty-foot rock bluff off to the left. In a swirl of dust, the SunFire came to a stop maybe ten yards away,

216

its headlights now lighting up the side of the truck.

Foley's black patrol car, its red-blue flashers still going, skidded to a stop ten yards from the SunFire, his headlights on the little Pontiac and the truck. He was over on the right edge of the road.

Gently but firmly pumping her brakes as she'd been taught to do in the pursuit driving class, Ro brought her Crown Vic to a stop five or six yards behind Foley, quickly turning off her headlights so as not to silhouette him. She was a little to his left.

Briefly flicking her eyes up to the rear-view mirror, she saw One-Four's red-blue strobes coming up from behind. One-Four doused his headlights, but like Foley and Ro left his light bar going; together the three patrol car's strobes splashed an eerie kaleidoscope of red, blue, and purple across the rock walls around the pond.

1:32:30 a.m. - As she glanced back at the pickup truck, the SunFire and the LLPD patrol car just ahead, Ro suddenly snatched her mic from its dashboard bracket and jammed her thumb down on the transmit button....

"Armstrong," she shouted, not waiting for an acknowledgment. "10-32!" — *man with a gun!*

About the Author

Dave Lager is the pen name of Dave Ramacitti, who at 75 is supposedly retired, except he very much looks forward to working on his Ro novels every chance he gets.

Ro's Handle is the first Ro Delahanty book; his second, *The Berlin Riddle*, is nearly done and there are nascent ideas for several more Ro stories.

Dave's career includes working as a newspaper reporter and magazine editor and publisher, and as a marketing-public relations consultant helping small business be more effective marketers. Under his own name he has previously published non-fiction books and manuals for the small business market, including: *Do-It-Yourself Publicity*; *Do-It-Yourself Advertising*; *Do-It-Yourself Marketing*; *So You Want to Own Your Own Business*; *The Three Marketing Absolutes: Know Your Customer, Know Your Competition, Be Unique*; *The Three Marketing Absolutes: A Step-By-Step Guide to Learning About Your Customers, Your Competition and Achieving Uniqueness In The Marketplace*; and *The All-Important Stuff You Gotta Do First to Effectively Market Your Small Business*.

He has been married to his best friend for 25years and has three grown stepchildren and seven step-grandchildren. He lives next to the Mississippi River in Rock Island, Illinois.

To learn more about Dave Lager and Ro Delahanty visit us at davelagerbooks.com…

And be sure to sign-up for our blog and like us on Facebook.

CPSIA information can be obtained
at www.ICGtesting.com
Printed in the USA
FFOW03n1106261117
43684210-42542FF

9 781629 897943